'. . . (1951–2) was a time of sheer and total happiness for me. But I felt it to be so brittle that I decided to exorcise its fragility by writing a tale. This was to be the last word in eroticism and sadism . . . like a kiss of peace bestowed on the principle of Evil.'

André Pieyre de Mandiargues

André Pieyre de Mandiargues

Portrait of an Englishman in his Chateau

Translated by J. Fletcher

Dedalus

Dedalus would like to thank the Burgess programme of the French Ministry of Foreign Affairs and the French Ministry of Culture in Paris for their assistance in producing this book.

Published in the UK by Dedalus Ltd, Langford Lodge, St Judith's Lane, Sawtry, Cambs, PE17 5XE

ISBN 1 873982 93 3

Distributed in the United States by Subterranean Company, P.O. Box 160, 265 South Fifth Street, Monroe, Oregon 97456

Distributed in Australia & New Zealand by Peribo Pty Ltd, 58 Beaumont Road, Mount Kuring-gai, N.S.W. 2080

Distributed in Canada by Marginal Distribution, Unit 102, 277 George Street North, Peterborough, Ontario, KJ9 3G9

Publishing History
First published in France in 1953
First published by Editions Gallimard in 1979
First English translation published by Dedalus in 1999

L'Anglais décrit dans le chateau fermé © *Editions Gallimard 1979*

Translation copyright © *Dedalus 1998*

Typeset by RefineCatch Limited, Bungay, Suffolk
Printed in Finland by Wsoy

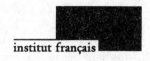

institut français

French Literature from Dedalus

French Language Literature in translation is an important part of Dedalus's list, with French being the language *par excellence* of literary fantasy.

Séraphita – Balzac £6.99
The Quest of the Absolute – Balzac £6.99
The Experience of the Night – Marcel Béalu £8.99
Episodes of Vathek – Beckford £6.99
The Devil in Love – Jacques Cazotte £5.99
Les Diaboliques – Barbey D'Aurevilly £7.99
Spirite (and Coffee Pot) – Théophile Gautier £6.99
Angels of Perversity – Remy de Gourmont £6.99
The Book of Nights – Sylvie Germain £8.99
Night of Amber – Sylvie Germain £8.99
Days of Anger – Sylvie Germain £8.99
The Medusa Child – Sylvie Germain £8.99
The Weeping Woman – Sylvie Germain £6.99
Infinite Possibilities – Sylvie Germain £8.99
Là-Bas – J. K. Huysmans £7.99
En Route – J. K. Huysmans £7.99
The Cathedral – J. K. Huysmans £7.99
The Oblate of St Benedict – J. K. Huysmans £7.99
The Mystery of the Yellow Room – Gaston Leroux £7.99
The Perfume of the Lady in Black – Gaston Leroux £8.99
Monsieur de Phocas – Jean Lorrain £8.99
Portrait of an Englishman in his Chateau – Pieyre de Mandiargues £7.99
Abbé Jules – Octave Mirbeau £8.99
Le Calvaire – Octave Mirbeau £7.99
The Diary of a Chambermaid – Octave Mirbeau £7.99

Torture Garden – Octave Mirbeau £7.99
Smarra & Trilby – Charles Nodier £6.99
Tales from the Saragossa Manuscript – Jan Potocki £5.99
Monsieur Venus – Rachilde £6.99
The Marquise de Sade – Rachilde £8.99
Enigma – Rezvani £8.99
The Wandering Jew – Eugene Sue £9.99
Micromegas – Voltaire £4.95

Forthcoming titles include:

Sebastien Roch – Octave Mirbeau £8.99
The Man in Flames (L'homme encendie) – Serge Filippini £10.99
The Woman and the Puppet (La femme et le pantin) – Pierre Louÿs £6.99
L'Eclat du sel – Sylvie Germain £8.99

Anthologies featuring French Literature in translation:

The Dedalus Book of French Horror: the 19c – ed T. Hale £9.99
The Dedalus Book of Decadence – ed Brian Stableford £7.99
The Second Dedalus Book of Decadence – ed Brian Stableford £8.99
The Dedalus Book of Surrealism – ed Michael Richardson £9.99
Myth of the World: Surrealism 2 – ed Michael Richardson £9.99
The Dedalus Book of Medieval Literature – ed Brian Murdoch £9.99
The Dedalus Book of Femmes Fatales – ed Brian Stableford £8.99
The Dedalus Book of Sexual Ambiguity – ed Emma Wilson £8.99
The Decadent Cookbook – Medlar Lucan & Durian Gray £8.99
The Decadent Gardener – Medlar Lucan & Durian Gray £9.99

THE AUTHOR

André Pieyre de Mandiargues was born in Paris in 1909. During the war he retreated to Monaco where in 1943 he published, *Dans les années sordides*. He returned to Paris at the end of the war. In 1947 after meeting André Breton, he became involved in the activities of the Surrealists. As well as being a poet and novelist, Mandiargues has written plays, essays and art criticism.

He won the Prix des Critiques in 1951 for *Soleil des Loups* and the Prix Goncourt in 1967 for *Marge*. His work has been featured in *The Dedalus Book of Surrealism* (Volumes 1 & 2), *The Decadent Cookbook* and *The Decadent Gardener*.

André Pieyre de Mandiargues died on the 13th of December 1991.

It is my particular wish that this book be thought of as a sort of bullfight.

To the memory
of E. J. and for
the Friends of the
Aubrey Beardsley
(secret) Society.

To be sexually attracted to highly refined pain is as natural to a man of healthy constitution as the tendency of a male rabbit to devour its offspring.

W. M. Rossetti
(in an essay on Swinburne)

ONE

'When you come to Gamehuche,' Montcul told me, 'check the time of the tides carefully. The access road is usually under water and only passable for an hour or two at low tide. I suggest you do the following: Buy a copy of the local paper, the *Phare de Vit*. It comes out every Saturday and gives you the times of high and low tide at St-Quoi-de-Vit for the entire week. If you add twenty minutes to the time given in the tidetable, you'll have the exact time of the tide at Gamehuche.'

I took care to follow these instructions and, having done my calculations, I expected to arrive while the tide was still going out. However, the poor state of the roads and the lack of signposts in that almost uninhabited part of Brittany delayed me to such an extent that it was fully three quarters of an hour after the tide had turned when I reached the beach where the causeway which led to the chateau began. I was none too happy about driving the car onto this narrow roadway, which could best be described as little more than an embankment. In the middle, the waves were already beginning to break over it. On the other hand, it was no more than a couple of kilometres to the chateau, which stood out amidst the waves as a dark mass against a still clear sky. So I put the car into gear.

In the past, travellers would have got to Gamehuche

15

either by boat at high tide or across the slippery rocks. I reckoned that the concrete roadway had been built about fifty years ago, although I know that the untrained eye has a tendency to overestimate the age of such constructions, those which succumb to the buffeting of the sea after a short space of time. It was clearly in urgent need of repairs, in addition to the more recent ones, traces of which were clearly visible beneath the young seaweed.

If the causeway had been any longer, I'd have thought twice about setting out. I had to be on constant look-out for various dangers: deep holes in the surface, which, with five or six pebbles in them, looked like a nestful of chickens eggs; cracks, thick with sea foam, which ran across the causeway from one side to the other, between parapets encrusted with shells; little pools lined with sand or gravel which made steering treacherous; rusty iron spikes which stuck out of the concrete all over the place and proved to be the greatest hazard.

The wall on either side was no higher than the car's hub caps, and at intervals along its length there were outlets. Whenever a wave broke over the wall the sea water spurted out through these holes in spluttering jets. Towards the end of the causeway the road rose quite sharply. This caused the wheels to spin. But there, once I'd got through the seaweed and the wet, I was relieved to see that I was now above sea-level. I stopped the car at the gates to the chateau, on a sort of platform which I think was well above the high water mark, except perhaps during the big equinoctial tides.

No sooner had I hooted the horn than I realised I was being watched. A dark shape moved behind a peephole. Then it disappeared. The door was half opened to reveal a superb Negro, built like an athlete. He was wearing old green velvet shorts over bare legs. His matching jacket had brass buttons with a device – a pair of buttocks – stamped on them. It was difficult to specify which century or which theatre company this character belonged to. He addressed me in a familiar tone.

'You must be Montcul's friend. You got here just in time.'

He pointed to the road I had come by. At that very moment, a wave crashed over the jetty in a huge joyful explosion of spume and spray. Others were building up behind it. Their high curves promised a display of similar verve and power.

'We were expecting you sooner,' he said. 'Bring your car into the courtyard.'

He opened the double doors. An incline of a few metres led into the courtyard, which was a little higher than the level of the platform.

Behind me I heard the sound of the doors, metal grinding against metal, as the iron joints made certain that the doors were shut tight. I switched off the ignition. The engine gave a little hiccough and fell silent, like when a heart stops beating. Somewhat dazed, I got out of the car and looked around at the place Montcul had chosen as his retreat and where he had told me to meet him.

First of all I should point out that the word 'chateau' failed to give an accurate description of the true nature of the place, although I must admit it was the word used by the few locals I came across on the moors when asking for directions. Gamehuche was actually an old fort (which must have often been used as a prison) and certainly predated the time of Vaubon. It probably fell out of use at the end of the Napoleonic wars. I had no idea of the extent of the changes it had undergone in the last period. It was built out of blue-black granite which was far too hard to be subject to patina or erosion, the two types of weakness which usually beset stone. This made it look new, so much so that it was practically impossible to tell the difference between the original construction and any whimsical restorations which subsequent owners had imposed upon it.

At first sight, the most striking feature was its unusual geometry whose laws it obeyed rigorously. From the outside, Gamehuche appeared to be a massive, squat tower completely devoid of windows. But what you saw, whether from the beach or from on board a boat out at sea, was only ever the outer wall, which was perfectly circular, smooth and even. If it hadn't been for its situation you might have mistaken it for the outside of an arena. But what sort of beasts might have fought there? What sort of people would have filled the seats – there among these sea mists and squalls, in this vast solitude of bare rocks pounded by the waves?

Within the defensive perimeter, a keep rose against one of the walls. In shape it was a slightly elongated oval. In addition there were six smaller towers. Two of these were at a tangent to the keep and along with it formed the main living quarters. Two others meanwhile stood at the edge of the diameter, parallel to the axis of these buildings, and the last two flanked the entrance gate. A single, narrow, first floor window, covered with a metal grill, set these last two towers apart from the rest of the buildings within the walls. Nearly all the rest of the available surface consisted of huge transparent bay windows. The stone did little more than serve as the frame to a vast expanse of glass. The roofs of this building were flat, which was uncharacteristic of the region, and leaded. They formed a terrace with a circular walkway. Nothing appeared above the height of the parapet, although on occasions you might have seen the upper half of an occupant of the chateau who had been tempted up there by the sunny weather, or for some other, less banal reason.

'Do you have any luggage? We'll have to take it up to the guest tower.'

The Negro's words reminded me of his presence. Perhaps he was irritated that my attention had been wandering up among the clouds buffeted by the wind and down amid the sound of breaking waves which were crashing onto the blocks of stone below the ramparts. I took two suitcases out of the boot to hand to him. He picked up one of them. Not wishing to make a fuss, I picked up the other one. But this insistence on equality between servant and master, combined with a certain arrogance of voice and gesture towards me was not done with the intention of making me angry. Quite the opposite. For it underlined the fact that when I stepped over the threshold of Gamehuche I entered an eccentric, sealed world which had different laws and customs to the one I'd just left behind. It also brought with it delicious benefits, and these I would learn about soon enough.

So I was about to follow this man, whom inwardly I was already calling 'my black brother', when the door to one of the middle towers (the one to the right of the main gate, to be precise) opened. In the doorway there appeared a vision which I found beguiling. It was a mullata girl (just turned seventeen, as I later found out) delightfully cat-like, or she-monkey, about the face which was a little smaller than normal in proportion to the rest of her body. Her nose was a little too short and her mouth a little too big. She opened wide her russet eyes and her skin was as smooth and as clear as could be. Her hair, curly rather than crinkly, fell to one side over the beautiful curve of her shoulder. She was dressed in a sort of bathrobe in coral-coloured satin edged with swan's down. This robe was very Louis XVI, with wide sleeves and a low neckline designed to conceal as little of her cleavage as possible. Her feet were tiny and she was wearing mauve shoes over white socks embroidered with red foxing.

'Hello, friend of Montcul,' she said. 'I'm Viola.'

'Good day, Madame Viola,' I replied.

She started to laugh, with all the charm of a puppy. Then she said:

'Just call me Viola. I will call you Balthazar. I like this name. It's a name I've given to all the men in my life I've ever been in love with. They were like brothers to me.'

I was surprised that my unexpressed thoughts found an echo in this, but I was by no means unhappy with an incognito which promised so much. I bowed to her wishes. However, I still had a question for her:

'What about Montcul? Do you call him Balthazar too?'

'Montcul is Montcul.'

The vivacity with which she replied gave me a first glimpse of the hitherto unseen delights of her bosom.

'Balthazars are Balthazars. One man's meat. . . But you don't need to concern yourself about such matters, dear brother Balthazar. Come. Let's go up to the guest tower. I'll put you at your ease.'

She took me by the arm and having done this, she used my hand to gently stroke her nipple through the material of her dress. I'd never realised that a nipple could be so pointed, for up until then I had only ever fondled the breasts of white women.

In this way we crossed the courtyard towards the other middle tower into which the Negro carrying my suitcase had already disappeared. The doorway was too narrow for the two of us to pass, so with great regret I had to disengage from the lovely Viola. However, as I guided her politely in front of me, I ascertained that her arse was no less well developed and firm than her breasts. We climbed a few steps and, pulling aside two large wall-hangings, we entered a circular room which was a bathroom. It was quite superb.

The middle of the room, at floor level, was taken up by a bath. In fact it was more like the basin of a fountain than a bath. The middle of the bath in its turn was marked at the water level, by a very large stone whose shape, to recall the 'rampant' heraldic device of the lord of Gamehuche, couldn't fail to surprise the unsuspecting visitor. More precisely, although it was probably modelled on waves, the stone bore a very close resemblance to the buttocks of a colossal Venus of the Caves. Two holes that had been made at just the right point in this stone provided hot and cold running water at will. And you could easily get out of your depth if you decided on a whim to have a little paddle around the stone near the hole which pissed out cold water, whereas near the source of the hot water, it was appreciably shallower.

The first of the two wall-hangings was made from blue gauze. The second, inside, was of that tough oilcloth, reddy-brown in colour, from which sou-'westers and tarpaulins for canoes are made. The latter hanging covered the whole ceiling and hung down to the floor behind three seats made of raw cork. It parted either side of the windows which were hung with the other, less weighty wall-hanging. This meant that the illumination of the room resembled that blue light which is found in caves by the seashore. Behind this double curtain, a spiral staircase fixed into the wall led up to the first floor.

We spent just long enough in the bathroom to cast an eye over it and admire it. Then we went upstairs, where we found the Negro relaxing on the bed.

'Gracchus,' said Viola. 'You may go. My friend Balthazar needs to rest.'

'Fine,' he replied. 'I see. It hasn't taken long for *him* to become a Balthazar.'

He got up, not without one or two further grumbles, and left via the opening in the floor. My mulatta friend closed the trap door behind him. We were alone.

The ceiling in the bedroom was much higher than in the bathroom. The room was also wider, since there was no space taken up either by the staircase, or by the sort of corridor which ran between the wall and the oilcloth curtain. From the ceiling hung two muslin drapes, white on the inside and light red on the outside. These were attached to the wall by a system of wooden spokes set halfway up a pole of natural pine. These supported its graceful gauze roof, like the canopy of a small portable seraglio. As with the room downstairs, but to a greater extent, daylight flooded in through a large bay window. The double screen of red and white tinged the light with the colours of the dawn. In the same way light is reflected off flesh which has been inflamed by the lashes of a whip. The pole stood at the centre of a huge circular bed which, with your head on a pillow around the shaft, could easily have slept eight people – even ten or twelve at a squeeze. The bed was covered with skins, long-haired, probably goatskins. These had been dyed vivid reds, violets and pinks. Other skins, short-haired sheepskin, which ranged in colour from washed-out pink to straw yellow, served as rugs placed between the bed and a divan which ran right the way round the room – except where the trapdoor to the staircase was. As with the bed, the divan was covered with goatskins whose colours went from a very, very dark brown to ochre to that almost white beige which is exactly the same colour as an Isabella horse. And over everything, mingling with the strong musky smell of the fleeces, drifted a thick heavy perfume like that of an oriental souk.

After she had pulled some of the neatly placed covers off the divan, Viola lifted a section of the bench which acted as the lid to a deep chest. This was where my suitcases had been deposited. She then arranged some cushions and sat me down comfortably on the bed. Kneeling in front of me she undid my shoelaces and eased off my shoes. She lifted my feet to her face and tickled then lightly with her eyelashes. Then she licked the soles and the gaps between my toes using her muscular little tongue. After this she joined me on the bed still wearing her robe which she had been unbuttoning from top to bottom while she was tending to my feet. I saw that she was completely naked except for her shoes. Her nimble fingers were expert at undoing me, and she did not stop until she had removed every stitch of clothing. She then lay on her stomach between my legs, supporting herself on her elbows. She looked up at me laughing and ran her pointed breasts all over my body. I must admit that my prick went as hard as a jackhammer. She indulged in a few more little gestures with her breasts and tongue. I closed my eyes in sheer delight. Then her head moved down my body and I felt her sucking me.

24

She latched onto the glans immediately without touching the shaft and she pulled on it exquisitely with little jerks. She nibbled at it skilfully, (in other words she never went beyond the point where pleasure gives way to pain). Sometimes she took me deep into her throat just behind her tonsils (which I bumped against and which, having overcome some resistance, I felt gently gripping my tool). This was an absolutely delicious sensation, especially since I'd got so fed up with being sucked by women who only used their lips, like whores.

It wasn't long before I ejaculated, this being the first time I'd emptied my balls in several days. Then Viola drew herself up towards me and kissed me, at the same time filling my mouth with some of the come I'd spurted into hers. It was our first and only lovers' kiss. We swallowed together in what might be described as an almost ceremonial manner.

'Ah, my dear Balthazar,' said Viola. 'Doesn't that bring us closer together than all the words under the sun? You are truly my brother now.'

She sighed heavily, which seemed to me was her way of covering up a burp, and she placed my penis back in her mouth. She sucked off any remaining sperm and licked it clean. Then she dried it by rolling it in the palm of her hands, like a cigar.

'You must be tired after your journey,' she said sweetly, seeing that I was failing to respond to her gracious gesture. 'You should have a little sleep. I'll come and get you in time for dinner.'

I'm not sure I'd have been able to get into the

circular sheets without completely unmaking the bed if my friend (or rather, my little sister) Viola hadn't taken hold of an edge to show me where the opening was.

I snuggled in. She pulled over me the hairiest and most colourful fleeces, like a heavy cloak of honour, before she left the room. I had no idea where she was off to, but as she disappeared through the trapdoor and down the spiral staircase I noticed that she hadn't bothered to do up her robe.

Left alone, I lay quite still waiting for the sleep she had advised me to take. It failed to arrive, however, so I began piecing together some fragments of memory.

TWO

The first appearance Montcul made in my life was while I was staying in Berne with an old girlfriend (by that I don't mean 'elderly') and with whom I was playing a game of long-distance hide-and-seek. I still look her up from time to time because she has small breasts which will never sag and her belly exudes a scent of vanilla and ambergris.

My girlfriend introduced this man to me under the name of Sir Horatio Mountarse, first secretary at the British Legation. I knew her well enough to realise that unless he was a man who had lost all interest in women, he'd been screwing her. However, as well as the pleasure of renewing an old liaison, the main reason for my stay in the Capital of the Swiss Bear was to have an old pocket watch of mine repaired. It was one I had a particular fondness for. Inside its case, when it's working properly, twelve mechanical schoolboys appear exactly on the hour. They present themselves with their shorts round their ankles to a schoolmaster who sodomises the requisite number of arseholes according to the hour on the dial. Now, it had been mended that morning, and as I had the watch in my pocket and it was time for tea, it gave me the chance to show off my little schoolmaster "striking five". The diplomat was lost in admiration for my curio.

'Are you an aficionado of the brothel?' he asked me.

'It's a good deal more interesting than solitaire or *jeu des graces*. But is there one, in this town of Protestants, with their frigid pricks and black feet?'

'Not officially, but if you'll allow me, this evening I'll take you to a certain establishment which I frequent. It's a place not entirely devoid of a certain charm.'

So Sir Horatio took me on an expedition to one of the lower class districts on the other side of the river Aar. We went down a stinking alley and stopped in front of a dark doorway. Here, he rapped out a long and complicated pattern of beats on the door with the ferrule of his walking stick. This was done so that I'd be able to remember the pattern in the future. The door was opened, the English diplomat was recognised and we were ushered into one of those 'lucky cowsheds'. These are to be found in great numbers in some of the more backward cantons of German-speaking Switzerland where none of the girls are particularly keen to make their cunt or arse available to all-comers.

Under a roof of large beams was a vast room with a white wooden floor. Around the walls of the room, I recall, were a series of square stalls each one of which contained a pedigree Emmenthal cow. The animal was provided with a thick bed of straw, but dirtier than might have been expected given its role. In the middle there were tables where the customers, of which there were a fair few that night, sat and drank beer from huge tankards. As soon as these were empty, they were refilled by serving girls who were perfect representatives of the Berne type. By that I mean they were round-bellied, with heavy pendulous breasts, fat arses and shapely legs – rather exciting, for all that they exuded an air of monumental stupidity.

'Try your luck. An ecu a go,' announced the owner, as he paraded from one table to the next an object which struck me as repulsive. It was the belly of an old doll which had been hollowed out like a piggy bank, its cunt edged with rabbit fur. Into this cunt, exactly the same size as a coin stamped with the head of William Tell, the revellers stuffed their cash.

Most of the time, absolutely nothing happened. (The owner of the cowshed did good business). However, now and again, after the insertion of a coin, a Swiss national flag would pop up from the navel. In this case, all the barmaids quickly gathered around the winner allowing him to choose one of them. Curiously, to my way of thinking, they stood with their backs to the winner. Although from the front they displayed the utmost modesty, buttoned up to the neck, at the back their dresses were lifted to reveal their buttocks, unimpeded by any underwear. Apparently, in German Switzerland the only thing a woman is judged by is her arse.

Having chosen his prize, the winner led her to a cowstall. Some closed the stall doors, which meant that during their 'private moment' all we could see were the upper parts of the cow. The majority, on the other hand, left the door wide open to besport themselves in front of their friends who were still at the table. They got undressed publicly, often hanging their trousers and shirt on the horns of the cow, then stripped the scrubber and fucked her underneath the belly of the bovine in full view of everybody. The cows remained placid enough. They were well and truly used to all this.

Sir Horatio and I tried our luck on a number of occasions, and I was the first to succeed in running the cross of Geneva up the flagpole. I plumped for the least buxom of the females, a choice which was loudly mocked by the drinkers. She was a real beauty, at least as far as her shape was concerned. But she shared with her peers such a thick hide that it felt more like running my hand over rind than over a woman's skin.

When the two of us were naked, I didn't shut the doors. I thought that in a gesture of gratitude for having brought me to such a delightful dive, Sir Horatio might like to watch me fucking.

It's a strange sensation to be lying totally naked, albeit with a really beautiful woman, stretched out on a bed of straw soiled with cow pats and urine, between the legs of a cow which could crush you or seriously injure you with one blow from its hoofs.

My companion (she told me her name was Litzi) made me lie with my face more or less directly under the animal's arse. While Mlle Litzi, who was positioned on top of me, energetically rubbed the rear end of the animal, I was fondling the swollen udder of this huge animal and amused myself by pulling on the teats and squirting warm, creamy liquid over the two of us.

Later on, Sir Horatio's flag went up, but he shut himself in very carefully and nobody could see how he took his pleasure with the young fat girl he had chosen. Some of the regulars, however, were heard to say that the cow had never been so upset. The diplomat emerged from the cowstall at the end of three quarters of an hour.

'I will let you see my prick another time . . .' he said to me. '. . . and when it's erect, which is a rare occurrence. I only did it today for a little amusement.'

The girl was dripping with cow piss. She was twisting her long, sponge-coloured hair to try and dry it out a little. But in vain. She was looking very put out, which was delightful to see, and it occurred to me that I'd been rather stupid with mine to find nothing better to do than ride the lazy bitch and shower us with milk. Sir Horatio was as buttoned up as ever, more like he'd just stepped out of a lavatory rather than a stable of whores.

Outside in the street, when I thanked him for an excellent evening, he invited me to pay him a visit the following year at his place, Gamehuche. He added that he was quitting the diplomatic service and as soon as the work on the old fort he'd purchased on the Breton coast had been completed to his satisfaction, he intended to retire there, to cut himself off from the world in order to pursue certain interests and studies.

'These may be of some interest to you,' he said again as we were about to go our separate ways. 'In fact, now that I know you, I'm sure they would.'

The war intervened, which meant that it was another eight years before we met up again. But we'd always corresponded by letter during that time – regularly, if not often. In one of his final letters he informed me that he'd changed his name – or rather that he'd translated it into French. Henceforth, Sir Horatio Mountarse would be known as M. de Montcul.

THREE

The light was fading and I was wondering if Viola had already forgotten about me when I heard the sound of her footsteps on the stairs. She'd changed neither her dress nor her shoes, but she'd carefully adjusted the former. She was also wearing a necklace of large golden flies threaded on a green ribbon. With her hair loose, her face delicately powdered with periwinkle, her lips the colour of cyclamen, I found her even prettier than before. She told me that we'd be dining in half an hour and that she'd take me down to the bathroom and watch while I bathed. She said she loved watching men at their ablutions.

After various remarks which never went much beyond pleasantries, we went back upstairs. I wanted to open my suitcase, but she wouldn't let me. Instead, out of another compartment in the divan-chest, she took a shirt with gathered flounces. It was made from the finest material I'd ever felt against my skin. This was followed by a pair of silk underpants, golden brown like the belly of a buprestis beetle. She helped me into a white cashmere dressing gown tinted pink, with large shawl lapels and a cord. Black hose and slippers with silver buckles completed my evening attire.

We crossed the courtyard — as a light rain was falling, Viola opened one of those outsized family umbrellas which hotel porters carry, in order to protect our glad rags – and entered the large oval building. We went into a dining room and there I immediately recognised Sir Horatio ... sorry, M. de Montcul who was dressed in an identical costume to mine, except that his was frankly much more salmon pink in colour.

'Good evening, Montcul,' said the mulatta girl, pushing me in front of her. 'Here's your friend, Balthazar. He gets a hard-on much quicker than you do. And his come tastes slightly of violets. It reminded me of a salad of young salmon.'

'It seems to me,' said my host, 'you've been gainfully employed since your arrival. No, don't apologise. It's no more than I expected of you. And allow me to go along with our pretty little Viola's whim and call you Balthazar also.'

I was not about to reject a name which had already brought me moments of such delight. Then M. de Montcul came up to me and continued:

'I'm absolutely delighted that you've accepted my invitation. I suggested, if I remember rightly, that you come and stay with me in a place which I humorously described to you as 'out of this world', and that there we might play certain games and carry out certain experiments. All the qualities Gamehuche possesses make it the ideal place for this. The night, the high tides, the currents which make the sea swirl and eddy around our ramparts, the huge walls, and the bolted doors at low tide, the deserted countryside inland, the suspicion which still clings to places with an infamous castle – all these things are enough to completely cut off our chateau from common humanity and to escape from their laws. You're the first person, other than myself and my four black companions, to come here of their own free will since I moved in. I should add immediately that you and I are the only ones who can leave when we like. Depending on the tide, of course. I've invited you here because at some point I realised that you're a serious man. I too am a serious man, in my own eyes. We both of us know that our type is in short supply in this world. In the main it was the frivolity and levity of everything out there that caused me to come and shut myself in here. For instance, I've hardly ever achieved an erection outside my own home. And is there any real point in getting a hard-on if you can't push things to their final conclusion? In my opinion, no. Especially as I'm of such an unusual nature, one which demands much more stimulation and effort to ejaculate and go limp than to go stiff. Here we'll indulge in the sort of game which suits the likes of you and I. But first of all I wish to acquaint you with our acolytes and our servants – the pawns in this game.

'Apart from you – henceforth, Balthazar – and I – you may call me simply Montcul – the chateau contains only two men. You've already met Gracchus the Negro, who's the valet when he has nothing better to do. The other Negro, Publicola, who is larger and much stronger than Gracchus, also acts as my valet, as well as my 'despatcher'. This is a delicate function which he performs superbly. You'll see later what this entails.

Given what you and I will be using the males for, there's little point in telling you their age. The same could not be said for the female pawns.

'Your friend, young Viola, she turned seventeen just twelve days ago. The very dark-skinned girl standing next to Viola who is looking at you and laughing – I wouldn't mind betting that the other has mentioned your prick to her – she's called Candida. She's nineteen and according to those who know about such matters, she has one of the most beautiful bodies of all black women.

'And this is Madame Edmonde, who admits to being thirty years old. She could best be described as a young woman of the world, and in that "world" she's renowned for having the most beautiful arse in Paris, and for knowing how to use it. Here we've put her to work in the kitchen, because that's her forte, as well as one or two other pleasant little duties which have made her almost indispensable to us.

'In a while you'll meet Mlle Luneborge de Warmdreck whose name we've changed to the rather more euphonious Luna. It's less effort on the vocal chords. She's the daughter of a Hanoverian Prince and is just over twenty. And the little one who's just coming in, is Mlle Michelette. She's thirteen and still a virgin.'

She looked at me with an expression of fear in her eyes. When she saw that Montcul had finished speaking, she bowed towards the two of us in the German courtly manner. It was at once both touching and ridiculous, given her situation. For this little girl was dressed like a cathouse whore. She tottered around on high heels. On her skinny little legs, she wore black stockings, held up around her buttocks by a flowery suspender belt embroidered with red silk poppies. The finer points of her slender, barely developed body, were easily discernible beneath the partly transparent veil of a dress shirt in crêpe de chine set off by frilly lace. The ribbon she wore round her neck was red like the flowers on her suspender belt. Her lipstick was applied thickly, and her eyes enlarged with make-up. Heavy mascara clogged her eyelashes, her eyebrows were lengthened with pencil and her cheeks rouged. Behind her appeared a big brunette, who was probably Luneborge de Warmdreck. In her hand she held a very supple fencing foil which whistled through the air as she brought it down hard on the little one's wrists in order to keep her away from us. There were some tears and a few drops of blood and through her stockings a gash in the living flesh which made you feel like biting the back of her neck or throttling her.

'Why must this little one always get under everyone's feet?' asked Montcul, who viewed this action with approval.

'Because she's got an itchy cunt. There's nothing more unhealthy than virginity. She gets scratches, scabs, cheese and rubbish down there. Creatures make their nests and lay their eggs in it. Cress grows there. One has to question your sanity, Montcul, in leaving her intact like this. We'll all end up with scabies and scrofula because of you and your virgins.'

Luna expressed herself with great vehemence, and

41

she was aided in the haughtiness of her speech by the singularity of her dress. She wore a long day dress in panther fur (or it could have been snow leopard, so pale and woolly was the skin). This she wore unbuttoned and unhooked, open from neck to hem. It allowed me to ascertain that the young princess had exactly the same colour pubic hair – somewhere between hazelnut and the colour of fallen leaves – as the hair on her head and eyebrows. This is unusual even among young women of noble birth. Her legs were bare. On her feet she wore golden sandals. Her toe nails, as with her finger nails, were painted mother-of-pearl.

'However, credit where credit's due,' she continued. 'I see that this little whore has gained some benefit from my teaching. Her curtsy was very well executed. Even my late uncle, who was a stickler for these things, couldn't have found fault with her! As a reward, this evening we might let her eat when she feels hungry. And even let her drink something. If Montcul will allow her to.'

She slapped the child hard across the mouth.

We couldn't wait to seat ourselves at the table. The two Negroes were busy pawing Edmonde's arse, while our host granted Michelette the favour that had been asked of him.

The room where we were dining was completely circular. Around us, under a ceiling of gilded wood, stood a circle of stone columns. What sort of stone they were made from I had no idea. It was smooth, fleshy and resembled pink-tinted wax. The columns were topped with large globes. They were close to the ceiling, although it was not actually resting on them.

The room was lit with candles and tapers. Their wax was the same crimson colour as the stone of the columns. They stood in chandeliers of varying sizes, decorated with images of girls being nibbled at by calves and fucked by donkeys. The wall was covered in a floating hanging material. It was a very heavy silk the colour of Rousillon wine. Currents of warm air which came from openings low down caused the hanging to ripple continuously and give off strange reflections. Between this wall and the colonnade there was a sort of circular gallery piled with animal skins, mainly bear and tiger, which formed sort of seats, or beds, or hairy benches. The floor in the middle was plain. It was either ebony or some other wood dyed black and waxed. Silver rings had been fixed into the floor and lying around were objects mostly of the same metal – stools, bowls, chalices. Also whips, sabres and dog collars.

The table was surrounded by three couches. (Another, of the same design, had been left in the gallery). These were curved, with room for three people and were scattered with cushions and bolsters in topaz satin. The frame of each couch was in silver and set upon castors.

As for the table itself, it was colossal and in the rocaille style. It was constructed out of hollow silver and warm water was pumped up from below through the foot of the table in order to warm it to blood temperature. There was neither table cloth, nor serviette. A large, well-wrought sculpture of obscene little subjects provided visual amusement amid the dishes, the decanters, the plates and the cutlery.

'If you need to wipe your mouth,' Viola said to me. 'You can use my hair or Candida's. And we'll do the same with yours.'

The negress and the mulatta had been placed on either side of me, by order of Montcul who was seated on the couch next to us between Luna and little Michelette. Edmonde was framed on either side by the two blacks, Gracchus and Publicola, although these three were perpetually running back and forth between the kitchen and the dining room to provide the food for the meal. So their couch was not often occupied.

The first dish, to all intents and purposes a soup, consisted of a large plate of "iced soft roe in the Priapic style". By this I mean that the roes, laid in a silver platter, were sprinkled with red pepper, grated ginger, saffron, castor sugar and an unknown blue powder which coated their surface in a multi-coloured fantasy. Above this shimmering rainbow, stood a stout prick sculpted in ice. It had enormous bollocks on which it had been mounted almost vertically. It looked like an anti-aircraft gun on its field carriage.

Edmonde was duly congratulated, for she was the one who had crafted this monumental work. But the congratulations turned into a slanging match over a suggestion which came from Luna that "the child should sodomise its mother". In other words, this masterpiece should be inserted into the arse of the artist, thereby achieving a total fusion between the object and its creator.

This idea met with the general approval of our little gathering. However, as we had need of the cook and there was a danger that the rest of the dishes would get burnt if she was not there to supervise, Montcul granted her a reprieve and ordered that the great cock be put in the fridge until the end of the meal so that its majestic dimensions might not be reduced in any way. His orders were carried out. Famished by the journey or perhaps by my amorous interlude, I had three helpings of the soft roes. Viola, on the other hand, ate next to nothing, which was no bad thing for her.

'It's good,' I said, 'Don't you like it?'

'Ugh! Fish spunk. And it's cold. Edmonde can have it. She's a stuck-up bitch. It's a man's come that I can't get enough of. You will give me some more of yours later, won't you, dear Balthazar?'

I assured her that she wouldn't go without, at some point, and I gently moved her hand which was blatantly fondling me.

'My dear little cocksucker,' exclaimed Montcul, 'Adorable fellatrix, charming little prick-eater, you will never go short of sperm. I will give you as many men to milk as you like. Your thirst ought to empty the balls of every man in the region, make the whole country sterile, desiccate all the whores and all the wives in the province . . . but, wait, here's a smell I recognise immediately. Ah, our favourite dish! *Béatilles de merde à la parisienne.* Fill your glasses. We have a very old château-châlons here. It's a wine which is so delectable that I couldn't imagine drinking it with any other sort of dish. I never eat shit without first proposing a toast to France. Vive la France!'

He knocked back his drink and we followed suit.

'The French are nothing but thieves who've gone around stealing everybody else's ideas,' Luna protested. 'Eating shit is a German invention. Before the war, you could get it in any good restaurant in Berlin.'

'I certainly agree that bird shit, or more precisely, tartine of snipe shit could be found, à la carte, at certain *wein* restaurants. But a good serving of human shit is as French as Béchamel sauce, Mme de Sévigné, the Légion d'honneur or the Concert Mayol. And I'm completely unbiased in this matter. After all I'm English, someone whose countrymen hold grilled cockroaches in the highest esteem. But if you want negress' shit, made into such smooth *béatilles*, you must admit that Gamehuche is the only place to find such a dish. Vive la France!'

He took another swig from his glass and choked on a little piece of turd, while young Candida watched him with a modest smile.

The shit was absolutely delicious. I helped myself to as much of it as I had the fish sperm. I would have taken more if the Negroes hadn't taken it away. The next dish to arrive was stuffed cow vulvas, I was reliably informed. From the gourmand's point of view, they were full of the most refined ingredients imaginable. Very white in colour and plump, they floated in a bone marrow sauce like little inflatable boats. To accompany them, we had giant asparagus. These Edmonde served to us one at a time with mock prudishness. When we'd consumed all that, the black waiters returned from the kitchen with two dishes of seabird brains. At first sight I was rather taken aback by their curious arrangement; for each brain, somewhere in size between a hazelnut and a walnut, had been stuck onto a beak. The idea was to pick up the little skull (which had been thoroughly cleaned), raise it to your lips and pull off the mouthful of brain which was crisp on the outside and a little raw in the middle.

'Go ahead, eat!' said Montcul, surprised by my reluctance.

'They're exceedingly rich in phosphorus, you know.'

I ignored his entreaty, however. The brains had an after-taste of fish oil which put me off. And I then began thinking, not without a certain unease, about the blood bath this dish must have entailed – several hundred seagulls killed for just two plates! And yet, why hadn't I considered that it must have required slaughter on a similar scale to provide one dish of vulvas? The reason, no doubt, was because I found the vulvas delicious, whereas the gull brains were disgusting. This opinion was not shared by the Negroes. They stuffed themselves with the brains more avidly than anything else.

When these dishes had been removed, Viola stuck out her tongue in such a way that it made my balls tingle and she informed me that dessert was about to appear. I assumed this meant fruit, gateaux and such like, but when I saw Gracchus and Publicola enter, staggering under the weight of an enormous dish, I wondered if I hadn't got drunk without realising it, or perhaps I was having some sort of mystical hallucination. Their dish was piled high with lobster, langoustine, crab and prawns. At moments it looked as if they were about to drop the lot (if this was just play-acting, we were certainly taken in by it) but finally they succeeded in placing the dish on the table. Nothing could have provided a more elaborate adornment for the silver table than this monstrous prickly bush made up of claws, humps, antennae and spikes. However, an even greater delight awaited us. The chef had removed the salty meat from these crustaceans and replaced it with confectionery. So, when we tore off a limb or cracked open a shell, we found inside crême bavaroise, citron and rose jam, chestnut purée, walnut, vanilla and chocolate paste, praline or coffee fondant, pistachio marzipan and sugar flowers. The pleasures of the palate were mixed with the delight of unexpected and heedless destruction. After a while (during which time I had consumed the contents of a small lobster, an edible crab, two velvet swimming crabs and a handful of prawns) the serving dish was almost empty. Nobody spoke during this course, except to announce, like in a card game, what we had in our hand. It was a veritable feast – but then, the voice of our host turned our attention to other matters.

'Edmonde,' he stated. 'If I were you I'd be stuffing myself less and thinking more about my arsehole. No matter that you've been put to the test by Caligula's weapon and every other cock that's visited this château! I tell you, taking a great prick made of ice in the arse is another matter. It's been known to split a person's guts.'

'Oh please, anything but that!' she begged. 'Punish me any way you wish, if you think I ought to be punished. Let me be buggered by everyone here, even the women, with those frightful dildoes of yours. Have me beaten. Bring in the dog. Anything you want, but spare me the ice.'

'You will be spared nothing. Have the great penis brought in immediately.'

While Gracchus went out to the refrigerator, our host turned to me and said:

'My dearest Balthazar, you'll be the one to perform this operation. The honour is yours as it's your first evening at Gamehuche. But above all, don't let this whore off lightly. I'll be most put out if you do. I was exaggerating just now when I said that she's almost indispensable to us. There's nobody here who couldn't be replaced from one day to the next, if that's our pleasure.'

It was a most gentlemanly offer, and I'd have liked to thank him in a similar fashion, but Gracchus had already returned with the great prick. My words were interrupted by cries of joy when this object appeared. It was lying in a long vessel lined with seal skin. This vessel in turn had been placed on a bed of crushed ice so there'd be no reduction in its size during preparations for its use. Wearing woollen gloves, I took hold of the prick by the balls and felt the weight of it in my hands. It felt like one of those wild west Colt 45s which can shatter an alligator's eye as effectively as a rifle. Viola lent me a little tape measure which, no doubt for shameless reasons, she kept in her stocking. With this I measured the tool before returning it to its cold store. Thirty nine centimetres long, with a diameter of twenty four centimetres in the middle and twenty five at the glans! Its dimensions made it a formidable weapon*. Meanwhile, Edmonde, realising that her tears were to no avail, gave herself over to our black waiters in preparation for the sacrifice.

Edmonde was a very beautiful woman, although her beauty was beginning to mature. Her hair was chestnut coloured, almost black, her eyes golden brown. Her skin was very smooth, and her upper lip was darkened by soft down. Her features and the rest of her body were classic. Her arse was totally spectacular. She was wearing a sort of full-length mauve shirt, with a long split under the arms so that her bosom and armpits were on public display. On her feet she wore green shoes with large rust-coloured irises. (Michelette was the only member of our little seraglio who was wearing stockings).

All that loveliness was placed at my disposal over one of the table sofas. This had been transformed into a sort of bench by dropping the back and one of the arms. The woman, on all-fours, was firmly attached by the wrists and ankles to the piece of furniture. An additional cushion placed under her stomach forced her to spread the cheeks of her arse

* Nature has improved on this, as can be seen in the Museum of Anatomy and Pathology at Strasbourg University. On display they have a forty two centimetres long prick, the possession of a drum-major in the Napoleonic army.

for me, something which she'd have found difficult to refuse.

I now had an operation to perform. I was given a knife and slit the dress from the hem to the waist. I then tore it left and right to expose her arse. It was ravishing. I had certainly noticed its shape already, but nothing about her face, shoulders or arms prepared me for the brilliance and whiteness of this arse from which the two domes stuck out majestically like a large ball of sugar under the curves of a narrow waist. It was without wrinkle or fold. Not one spot spoiled the admirable roundness of it. In its smoothness and firmness it resembled the purest marble, which brought to mind certain Italian cathedrals. These were truly the most sublime buttocks I had ever gazed on! Between them, was a very black fur, not unlike astrakhan, which clearly demarcated the beginnings of the buttock line.

In order to impart a little colour to the beautiful pale globes, I spanked them lightly a few times. This produced the desired effect. And I readily succumbed to the temptation to plant a kiss on the lovely arsehole which presented itself to me.

'Don't hurt me too much.' I heard her say, albeit in a whisper. 'I'll be all yours – whenever you want, however you want.'

But the nature of the offer, given the position that the seller found herself in, was so comic that I couldn't help laughing. At the same moment, Montcul encouraged me to 'plunge it in without any preparation'.

I picked up the huge prick of ice and took a firm

grip on it. I placed the tip in the middle of the arse-hole. Immediately it puckered up and the rose bud which had opened up the touch of my kiss con-tracted as if a string had been pulled tight. (It also reminded me of a sea anemone closing up). Then her cheeks began to tremble slightly and she got goose flesh on her thighs.

I tried to penetrate her by twisting the prick like a corkscrew, but the skin of the anus stuck to the ice, twisted with it, and that simply made the hole shrink more. In order to detach my instrument, I pulled it back with a quick movement. Edmonde whimpered and I saw a drop of blood on the glassy glans of the penis.

'Push it in,' said Montcul. 'Don't let the prick melt.'

Then he addressed Edmonde:

'Just open up your arsehole. It'll go in by itself.'

This time, following the orders I'd been given, I pushed the instrument forcefully. In contact with the cold object, the muscular contraction was so strong that all I managed to do was make her bleed more. Her complaints turned into cries of pain.

'Scream as much as you like, you stupid wretch,' said Montcul. 'It'll take more than that to give me an erection.'

As far as I was concerned, on the other hand, it was more than enough. My prick was standing to attention in my shorts, and Viola was stroking it with her hand as if it were a ferret. However, as the arsehole was resisting all my efforts to penetrate it, and the instrument had torn away a strip of pinky tissue which was probably intestinal mucus membrane, my friend went over to the table to get an oil jar, to avoid further damage being caused. She handed it to me despite the cries of protestation from the master of the household.

When I'd poured some oil over the arsehole and down her crack, I pushed in my index finger which was also covered in lubricant. The effect was extraordinary. As soon as it sensed that here was an object of flesh and bone, and not frozen liquid, the rosebud unfolded, opened up like a mouth, and grabbed my finger rather than resisting the pressure. I fistfucked her so as to give her insides a good oiling. Then I poured what was left of the oil onto the great penis. Holding her arsehole open with one hand, I drove the instrument brutally into her rectum with the other. The victim screamed again, her body twisted on the bench and her thighs trembled. I'm sure she was in a great deal of pain. In any case, her anus was spread open much wider than it had ever been by a Negro's cock or the biggest turd, and the sphincter latched furiously onto my ice battering ram. Taking advantage of the recent oiling and to make sure that if I stopped moving the penis it wouldn't get stuck to the mucus membrane again, I pushed the instrument in mercilessly until the bollocks were nestling in the flesh of the buttocks.

'There,' I said, getting to my feet. 'It's done. The Cyclops is blinded.'

Montcul added:

'Your operation has been most successful. But the wretch was lucky to have had you in charge of it. If it had been me, I wouldn't have behaved in such a gentlemanly manner. When it comes to salad, she can dress it however she wants. But if I'd been dressing her, I'd have used vinegar, not oil.'

Poor Edmonde! Everyone's attention was riveted on your arsehole. They all wanted to appreciate your suffering in the minutest detail and as your cries turned to the rattle of an animal with its throat slit, as little by little under the searing internal pain you began to lose consciousness and your body took on the soft chalky-white appearance of a fresh corpse, we watched a thin trickle of blood and water run between your buttocks and wet the material of the bench. The sight of this 'little death' produced such a furious urge in me that I had to push Viola's hand away from my prick so as not to come in my pants like some dumb idiot. I looked at the women around me and wondered whether I should come into some arse or mouth or cunt instead. Then I heard a peal of laughter, crystalline and daft, the sort that greets the school mistress when she breaks her glasses. It was Michelette, who having been given permission to eat and drink, had gorged herself to the point of almost passing out and was beside herself with joy.

'Edmonde's got an ice cube in her bum and she's all white,' she shouted loudly between fits.

'This little girl's very jolly,' said the German woman. 'She's making more noise than any of us.'

'My dear,' said Montcul. 'You've been trained as a kindergarten teacher in your own country, can't you come up with an effective way of dealing with noisy children?'

Behind Montcul's back, the German woman hit Michelette hard on the back of the neck with the foil. Then she whispered a few words in our host's ear.

'Fuck me!' he exclaimed, 'This is a turn-up. The little whore is showing some taste. And that's the last time I make fun of nursery schooling, if those are the methods they use!'

He twisted Michelette's nose spitefully and pushed her, sobbing, into the arms of the two Negroes. He ordered them to take her into the Aquarium room forthwith.

This trio led the way, followed by Montcul and Luna de Warmdreck, then myself flanked by the mulatta and the negress. We left the lovely Edmonde to digest her ice in peace. I hoped that there'd be pleasure in store and that I'd have the chance to deposit a quantity of sperm somewhere.

On the ground floor of the adjoining tower, there was another round room, like the bathroom through which I had to pass to get to my bedroom. Set into the walls at about chest height all the way round the room were the aforementioned aquaria. These were separated the one from the other by a simple row of pebbles. The fish tanks were dimly lit from behind by lamps which glowed through a screen of greenish water. Inside, fish and all sorts of marine life proliferated among the little mossy rocks, the shells and the fronds of algae which approximated to the sort of seascape visible through the glass of a diver's mask. Oxygen bubbles rose continuously to the surface of the water.

Just as in my bathroom, the centre of the room

was dominated by a circular bath. This one, however, was covered by a brass grill and the water was no more than a few inches deep, with a bed of sand and gravel. There were twenty or so octopuses lying in this shallow water, although most of them were no larger than those that get pulled out of holes in the rock on certain beaches in Normandy and Britanny, and whose presence is marked at low tide by a necklace of pebbles. The two or three largest, however, had tentacles almost as long as a woman's arm. Several had emerged from the water to cling to the grill. Luna de Warmdreck prodded them with her foil causing them to drop back into the water.

She told the Negroes to lift off the grill.

When her orders had been carried out, she turned to Michelette, who had been stunned by a couple of brutal slaps.

'Take a good look, you irritating little shit,' she said. 'You're going down into this hole. That'll teach you to laugh and make a noise when the grown-ups are talking. The octopuses are going to jump all over you. You're going to feel them bite you and suck your blood.'

Michelette struggled fearfully and screamed between choking on her tears. She shook the German woman's arm in a bid to escape, but Gracchus and Publicola had a firm grip on her. (I noticed they were both erect and were running their large black hands roughly over the tenderest parts of the little girl's body). They tossed her into the middle of the pool and immediately placed the grill back on top.

The octopus, freshly caught, were certainly alive.

I'd even go so far as to say that they were bloody lively. At first, when Michelette fell into the midst of them, they fled to the edge. But we ushered them back into the middle. The grill was far too low for the little girl to sit up, let alone stand up. She rolled around underneath it as if possessed by a demon. The very fine slip she was wearing was being torn to shreds, and she scraped her face and hands against the metal. Her whole body was covered in scratches. Terrified by the thrashing of the intruder, the octopuses were swimming from one side to the other with furious jerks. They squirted ink into the sand and into the water. They attached themselves to the little victim by lashing their tentacles round her arms and legs. Not that these creatures are as dangerous as many claim, but the embrace of their eight legs, the suction from the suckers with which they're armed, is severe. And when they sink their horny mouths, like parrot beaks, into the skin of a child, the bite they give is not exactly playful.

As far as we could gather, Michelette was completely off her head – lying on her back with her hair in the water, her legs wide open and her knees bleeding as they scraped against the metal grill. In this position, one of the utmost immodesty, she was exposed to our sight better (or worse) than if she'd been naked, as some scrap of crepe or lace still bedecked her bruised and filthy body here and there. Five octopuses had latched onto her and were not budging. Their tentacles were tightly bound round the flesh of her hips, belly and thighs. Another – one of the largest – was clinging to her face. She

57

appeared to be wearing a terrifying and burlesque mask. This tangled mass of childish flesh and cephalopod, set against a background of torn silk and lace, blood, animal ink, sand and salt water all together reached such heights of grandiose bestiality that it partook of what is obscurely referred to as *the sublime*. And I got completely carried away by it.

I grabbed hold of Viola, ripped off her bathrobe and pushed her forward over the grill. However I didn't have time to fuck her in the arse, because others were also beginning to feel the effects of the spectacle.

'By all the arseholes in heaven and on earth!' cried the master of Gamehuche. 'I think I'm getting a hard-on!'

The women around him pressed forward and Viola, who had escaped my clutches, gripped by fear, the moment she heard him speak these words, lost no time in helping him out of his clothes.

Stroked by breasts and buttocks, tickled by eye-lashes, caressed, sucked, Montcul's penis was soon standing to attention. It was a very pretty piece of work. Not monstrously long – according to Viola's well-tutored eye, it measured only about nine inches – but it was strikingly thick in profile, and was tipped by enormous crimson glans, which were seven inches in diameter. Its most remarkable feature was a lace-like membrane, the colour of pink and violet marble, which hung beneath it from the tip to the scrotum. This resembled the crest of certain reptiles.

I haven't seen many men erect as I'm neither a pederast nor much of a one for group sex. So I can't say for sure if this magnificent ornament – M. de Montcul's pride and glory – was unique or not. Certain doctors I consulted later assured me it was. So I have to take their word for it. As for the rest of his body, my friend was like a Bacchus, covered in hair which was somewhere between chestnut and ginger in colour, in contrast to his face which was close-shaven and cold, like a clergyman.

'Take the grille off. Quickly,' he shouted. 'The little whore is done to perfection, stewing in her own juice like that. I'm going to fuck her from behind and in front, and damn me if I'm not going to shoot my load!'

The grill was removed. Montcul, aided by the German princess and Viola who held him under the arms, leapt into the pond with the smack of a salmon leaping a dam, and we were all spattered with filth.

The octopus got more and more agitated, as if they were swimming in water which was too hot for them. We had our work cut out pushing them back in as they tried to climb out of the pool. One wrapped itself around the Englishman's heel. Another clung to the back of his neck. But he, without bothering to rid himself of them, seized hold of Michelette and hung on with fury. He grabbed her cruelly by her little breasts and buttocks, at the same time biting with all his strength at the large octopus which had latched onto the child's face. Two others, smaller in size, were fixed onto her thighs, barring his way to her virginity. He tore them off and we watched as he thrust his thumbs into their sack-like bodies and turned them inside out like a glove, spilling their guts out. He took these guts and rubbed his prick and balls with them. Then he returned to his victim. A series of strange sounds emanated from his mouth, among which I thought I heard a death rattle. He placed her in a suitable position and without any preparation other than that provided by the octopus entrails, with a single irresistible thrust, he plunged his tool into the young virgin up to his balls.

Michelette, having regained her senses, let out a piercing scream. I think Montcul must have done her some serious damage with his enormous cock for a cloud of blood began to drift through the ink-coloured water. But he continued to thrust in and out of her cunt for another twelve minutes or so without showing the slightest mercy.

When he pulled out – he had still not ejaculated – his penis presented a terrifying sight. A bloody drool hung from every point of the crest underneath. It was how one might imagine an iguana would look after it had taken part in some filthy ritual.

He returned to the child to rupture her arsehole with as much brutality as he had visited upon her cunt. He thrust in and out of her anus furiously for even longer. Finally, accompanied by a variety of cries, he turned his victim's head round and again began biting at the large squid which still cover her face like a mask. With his teeth, he tore out one of the creature's eyes, which shook and thrashed its tentacles like the rays of an artificial sun. Only then did he ejaculate, and he must have come pro-digiously because it lasted several minutes and was accompanied by spasms which shook his entire body slumped in the pool.

When he staggered to his feet, swaying, soaked in red and black from head to toe like an Indian god in his death painting, with his prick still stiff and several squid stuck to him here and there, he presented an awesome, magnificent sight.

'There!' he said. 'I need to be served up these little whores with a splash of sauce and some garnish. Now you'll understand why I've never shown the slightest weakness for their attractions outside my own house.'

His departure was majestic. He left us, followed by Candida whom he'd summoned with a click of his fingers. Behind the glass of the aquarium, the conger eels snaked back and forth and the blue fish attacked one of their number, a sick one.

My penis had been rock hard since the end of the meal and it was high time, I thought, to consider emptying the contents of my balls. With this praiseworthy intention in mind, I grabbed hold of Viola, who was masturbating next to me on the edge of the pool. As far as the young German princess was concerned I had little idea just how close her links were to the owner of the Chateau of Gamehuche. Of course, I'd never do anything which might make him jealous. Besides I preferred Viola the mulatta. But she'd just finished well and truly frigging herself and she gently pushed me away, panting.

'You know you can have me whenever you want, little brother,' she said. 'But my pussy's got so wet, it's exhausted. Wouldn't you rather take the one part of this little darling's virginity that's still intact? Her mouth!'

It goes without saying that this suggestion was more than I could have wished for. We dragged Michelette out of the pool then we covered it over again after we'd thrown back four or five octopuses which still clung to her arms or were crawling around at the foot of the fish tanks.

The child seemed to have fallen into that state of enfeeblement and languor which normally follows on from frenetic activity. Her haggard look, her gormless gaze, her livid complexion, continuous shivers, covered with ink and blood like the body of her torturer, everything about her increased my level of excitement.

'On your knees, filthy pig.'

The order came from Luna whose role in the debauchery which took place at Gamehuche was that of master of ceremonies.

'Open your mouth,' (Luna was rubbing herself under her dress). 'And if by any chance you bite M. Balthazar, or spit out anything of what he's going to spurt into your mouth, I'll put you back in the octopus hole and leave you there all night on your own, and in the morning all that'll be left of you will be a pile of bones.'

Publicola, the Negro was assigned to hold the girl for me between his legs. He forced her to her knees with her hands pinned behind her back. The black pig, he had a stiff prick which he rubbed against the back of the child's neck with small movements of his pelvis. The German woman and Viola were sitting on the grill masturbating each other. They'd positioned themselves so as not to miss any of the operation I was about to carry out.

I took hold of her head by the hair – which I think I mentioned had been bleached preposterously and cut in the style of Joan of Arc – and I gave her a beating about the eyes with my penis, which in terms of length and stiffness compared very favourably with a field marshal's swagger stick (and others things). My member seemed so engorged that I dared not prolong my amusement for fear of premature ejaculation.

The victim, whose face was already hideously swollen by the bites of the squid, opened her mouth at the level of my groin with an air of resignation about her, like one faced with the dentist's instruments. She stuck out her little pink tongue. Then without further ado I brutally stuffed my prick in. Holy God, what a sweet sensation! My only regret was that I didn't manage to give the novice more of a going-over. I was working hard to fill her throat, with such enthusiasm I was in danger of swamping her glottis and permanently stretching her larynx. She put up with all this without complaint – and for a good reason. Almost at once, unfortunately, I ejaculated. Pressing her face into my groin as she tried to pull away, I grabbed a handful of her fair hair, nearly pulling it out of her head, and pinched at her ears without mercy. At the same moment, Publicola's black pudding shot a torrent of spunk over the back of her neck and shoulders. The sperm that issued from the big black man was thick and warm, and it had an odour of common animal skins about it which was almost overpowering.

'Make sure you swallow it all,' said Luna, who was leaning forward towards the three of us. She was still being fingered by her girlfriend and was no doubt creaming herself like a vineyard snail.

'If you leave one drop, you're in for it.'

With an effort bordering on the heroic, the child obeyed. I pulled out, satisfied, my clothing stained with squid ink.

'Clumsy little bitch,' shouted the German woman, the moment she noticed the stains caused by my coming into contact with the victim.

'When is she going to learn not to rub herself up against people and make them all dirty. She's going to be punished properly this time. You two, take her into the dining room and tie her to the dog rings.'

Gracchus and Publicola took hold of the girl again. By now she was too stunned even to cry.

Meanwhile, Montcul had rejoined us. He'd been washed and dressed by the solicitous Candida. He was lightly powdered, scented and his hair was brushed back in waves.

'You bastards,' he greeted us in a tone of praise. 'You've been fucking without me.'

When Mlle de Warmdreck informed him of the orders that she'd given, he expressed his whole-hearted approval.

'We're too easy on children. Take this little one, for example. If you, my dear esteemed friend, weren't there to correct her when she misbehaves, we all know she'd crap on my head and then eat her own shit. I'm not saying that would be entirely disagreeable, but there's a time and place for everything. And the wonderful thing is that this is just the right moment for some doggy business. I just love it and we've deprived ourselves of that particular pleasure for far too long. I'm sure our friend Balthazar will enjoy this too. Come along then. The Negroes will have finished the preparations.'

We returned to the dining room. Edmonde was still there on the bench in exactly the same position that we'd left her before we paid our visit to the octopus pool. Her arse dominated the middle of the circular room with splendour beyond compare. Under the piece of furniture was a small pool of blood-stained water. This was all that remained of the magnificent instrument with which I'd pleasured her. The beautiful Edmonde had revived. Her rosy complexion, her sparkling eyes showed that she'd come to no harm in absorbing the enormous phallus and that when she wanted or indeed when the opportunity presented itself, she was capable of taking another, this time even more colossal. This was a measure of the extent to which this enchanting young woman could adapt herself, almost miraculously, to the act of sodomy.

She smiled sweetly at me as I passed and asked me to move the bench a little. She didn't want to miss anything of what Michelette was about to undergo. I complied with her wishes. I then saluted her, as I'd done before, by licking her arsehole. This seemed to me a wholly appropriate gesture to one of her character and in her situation – the equivalent of kissing her hand, if you like.

The others were seated as if at the theatre, on benches set out in a semicircle. In front of them, on the floor, I saw Michelette on her hands and knees looking for all the world as if she was about to play the sort of game that kids of her age play. But I noticed she had a collar pulled tightly round her neck. It was a large dog collar, with silver spikes and tufts of thick hair. A short chain from the collar to a ring fixed into the floor prevented her from standing up. Against the dark wood floor, this body of a child who'd reached puberty too young, with her almost white hair, her make-up smeared all over the place, with the bruises and filth which covered her, she looked a delightful little whore. Despite the fact that I'd only just come, and that I had no idea what was in store for her, simply looking at her was enough to induce a violent stiffening in the so-called noble regions of my anatomy.

'There! Very nicely arranged, you little tart,' said Montcul.

'And do you know what we have in store for you?'

'Yes, she does,' replied the German woman. 'She was present, and she enjoyed herself, when Baroness Sephora had a turn at this. But woe betide her if she doesn't stay on all-fours and play the bitch. She'll have me to answer to, and she knows how good I can be . . .'

'Let's get on with it,' said the master. 'The child will get tired in that uncomfortable position if we don't give her a little exercise. Publicola, bring

Nelson and Wellington in. And one of you others, I'd be most grateful if you'd bring me my great big wicked powder box.'

After a brief search through the coffers and under the fur-strewn beds, Viola was the first to present him with a certain container. When he'd opened the lid to show me the contents I saw inside a brown powder which resembled snuff.

'It's dog bait,' he replied. 'You can buy it in any shop which sells 'traps and baits'. In other words, it's made from the secretion of bitches in heat, which is dried and then ground into powder. It beggars belief that certain drugs such as opium and hashish, which after all carry little risk, have been subjected to the strictest regulation making them practically impossible for the average man to get hold of, while this concoction, which is more subversive than a call to man the barricades, is freely available everywhere. It just goes to show what an ass the law is in this respect. Imagine what a scandal would result if a few pinches were spread among a civil or military parade, a state funeral, the trooping of the colour, a visit by a foreign head of state, national sporting events . . .! Mind you, Rabelais wrote about just such an event. He provided an excellent illustration of how my instrument of profanation could be used, and I'm convinced he tried it out himself. Read it yourself. Or rather, re-read it. Chapter 22 of the second book. You'll find a highly instructive lesson in how to use dog bait for the purposes of public depravity. But for the moment, let's see what private depravity it can be used for.'

Through the half-opened door, the Negro announced that the dogs were ready.

'Good,' continued Montcul. 'Keep them chained up a little while longer. I'll call you when the bitch is ready. Bring Nelson in first. The other one will come on second.'

Montcul continued his explanation.

'Nelson fucks and Wellington buggers. At least that's how I've trained them. I'm also responsible for their names. They were handed over to me by the Resistance, along with a German officer. Unfortunately he failed to survive some of the experiments I inflicted on him and I didn't have the presence of mind to ask him their names. When they arrived here of course they couldn't do anything.'

Then he turned to Viola.

'Time to do your duty. This is a task which is customarily entrusted to your dainty little hands. The dogs know you. They love you. They become erect just by getting a sniff of your scent. This is because you've masturbated them so often as part of your official duties, or merely for the fun of it.'

He handed the powder box over to the mulatta who bent down towards Michelette's rear end. At the same time, I leant forward in my seat so as to savour every moment of increasing torment inflicted on the unfortunate victim.

My girlfriend gently stroked the girl's rump, just as one does to get she-goats to lift their tails and expose the vessel which nature dedicated above all to bestial practices. Viola ran her hand along the ridge between Michelette's cunt and arsehole. Then with great care, so as not to spill any, she took a little powder between her fingers and pushed it into the still bloody cunt. Heedless of the moans, she methodically anointed the labia as well, before wiping her hand on the buttocks. Then she shut the lid of the box and withdrew from the child on all-fours.

'Nelson . . . 'shouted Montcul.

Towards us rushed a mastiff, a huge specimen of his breed. Its smooth coat was light grey, a rather sinister colour, which was rendered perfectly by the word "*wan*", precisely the same colour as dirty chalk. Its ears, clipped into points, were pricked up like stocky little horns. Below them its eyes were pale green, and reflected the light from the candle flames, like cats' eyes. It came to a halt in the middle of the room and sniffed, while a trail of drool hung from its mouth. Its prick was stiff and the glans, deep red in colour, stuck out from a hairy sheath.

'These creatures get erect devilishly quickly,' observed Montcul, who came out with more comments than a pantomime showman. 'What's more, this one's got a member big enough to make most men envious. By that I mean most *white* men.'

For the group I was sitting with the dog showed nothing but contempt. Disappointed by our scent or our immobility, the ferocious animal first of all jumped up on Viola. She was the only one standing and had handled the extract of bitch too much to be able to get rid of every last trace. It put its paws on the woman's shoulders, like a giant inviting her to dance. This made her stumble backwards, but she managed to stay on her feet and it began thrusting back and forth, fucking with its prick at the bird feathers which bordered her robe.

'Get down, Nelson,' said the intrepid beauty. 'I've got something much better than me for you this evening. Go and screw the little girl. Good dog.'

Effortlessly, she freed herself from its clutches and pushed it, growling, over to Michelette. No sooner had it caught a whiff of the parts that had been sprinkled with powder, than it leapt on the girl grasping her flanks between its paws. It began fucking with such rhythmic force that I'm sure if any of my readers had been subjected to this ordeal they couldn't have endured it.

Viola stroked the beast in the same way she had caressed Michelette's rump. Then her fingers, long and slender, took hold of its enormous cock and guided it to the girl's cunt. It slid in first time, like a spoon into the belly of an overhung partridge. The mastiff thrust vigorously for four or five minutes. During all this time its mount seemed to display no reaction at all, other than a few little starts of pain. (However, it occurred to me that if we'd had a mirror placed in front of us, it might have shown the face and perhaps the expression of the victim.)

Then the beast stopped and a dumb look crossed its face while a stench of the kennel filled the room. Gracchus arrived to grab him by the scruff of the neck and pull him off. With terrible tugs the dog was pulled forcibly out of her cunt while Michelette, who was being half strangled by the collar round her neck, screamed blue murder. Blood flowed again from her cunt which had been torn by the entry of the dog's prick.

'England forever!' said Montcul, drinking a glass of gin mixed with piss, courtesy of the Princess de Warmdreck.

'Now, seeing that the Navy's a spent force, let's bring in the Army. Send for our glorious number two.'

The "great big wicked powder box", entrusted to Viola once again, performed its duty. Nelson, by now in a pitiful condition with his prick flaccid, was chained up again. Then through the door came Wellington and I must admit I was terrified. This beast, bigger and more abrupt than its companion, was black from head to tail, except for its fangs which were very white, and also its gums, tongue and prick, which were the same red as extract of wine lees. Its cock was as stiff as a board from the moment it entered the room, either because it was excited by the scent it had sniffed under the door, or because it was well used to this canine ceremony. It ran straight past Viola and headed for the girl. It grabbed her between its front paws just as Nelson had done, but it displayed no more skill at finding the place into which to stuff its member. As it struggled in a rather clumsy manner, although with a great deal of spring in its thrust, Viola was again called upon to guide it to the threshold of the temple in which it was to make its offering.

It encountered a certain resistance as it slipped into her arsehole up to its bollocks. It thrust so deep however, that it would completely have filled the arsehole of one of those Merino sheep which, in Beziers they say, are the most stubborn.

The child never stopped struggling and screaming from beginning to end. She seemed to have become totally unhinged. But even in her madness she still obeyed the orders she'd been given, remaining like a bitch, on all-fours. When the dog shot its load, most probably it bit one of her ears cruelly. After this, just like its predecessor, it fell into a sort of stupor.

The girl's sphincter was so tight and the dog's prick had swollen to such a size inside her back passage that all attempts to separate them would have been in vain if a large bucket of cold water hadn't been produced. The contents were tossed over the miserable couple and they were parted. The Iron Duke then went off to join Lord Nelson.

'This girl's been well and truly deflowered,' said our host by way of conclusion.

Nobody said anything in response. We felt so empty (or contented) that it was as if we'd climaxed along with the dogs. Then our host went on, addressing himself to Gracchus and Publicola.

'Take her away, you two. Enjoy her, in whatever way you wish. But make sure you get rid of her before dawn. I never want to see or hear of her again.'

'I think you should entrust that task to me,' said Luna, who had got up at the same time as the Negroes.

Luna followed them as they dragged their victim screaming from the room. She had a strange smile on her face, somewhere between the demented and the triumphant.

A few moments later, more to break the silence than out of curiosity, I asked:

'So, who's this Baroness Sephora you were talking about a little while ago?'

'Oh,' replied Montcul. 'She *was* a person of no great interest. Austro-Polish and the wrong side of fifty. She was terrified of the German police, so she'd taken refuge with some of the chaps in the Resistance. It was they who handed her over to me. She put on airs, which were totally baseless, babbled on about theosophy, claimed that she only ate raw eggs, dairy products and honey. And as she pretended to hate all animals, and dogs in particular, rather like Restif de la Bretonne, I thought it'd be entertaining to have this old bag fucked by my mastiffs. But the most amusing part of this story was when she refused go down on all-fours, ready for martyrdom as it were. She was terribly concerned to maintain her "dignity as a human being". She rolled around on the floor, stark naked, her thighs, which were pure cellulite, trembling like wet curtains. To make the bitch perform we had to attach her by the hands and feet to the rings you see here, as well as using the collar which was all that Michelette required. We also had to put a bunch of acacia branches under her belly. You should have seen the arsehole she presented to Wellington after she'd been sprinkled with powder. What nuptials! The harlot would have asked for more . . . but, you must excuse me, I feel very tired all of a sudden. I blame that little tramp they're in the process of 'despatching'. Would you mind very much if we continue with this

73

conversation tomorrow? For my part, nothing would give me greater pleasure. Meet me on the ramparts of the chateau, about midday. We'll chat and look at the sea before luncheon.'

I accepted the invitation and wished my host goodnight. He went off to bed. We set Edmonde free who was whimpering under her bonds. Then I made my way to my bedroom in the company of Viola and Candida. In the great round bed we played sex games long into the night before succumbing to sleep, deep post-coital sleep, peaceful and restorative, which truly deserves to be called the 'sleep of the just' or 'sleep of the innocent'.

Four

When I awoke (for the first time, I might add) it was light and I was alone in the circular bedroom. The disarray of the sheets close by, stiff with dried spunk, bore witness to the fact that I hadn't dreamed the events of the night before. I also knew that if I left the room and then returned to it, I'd be overcome by the pungent odour which black women leave behind when they spend the night in a confined space. I decided that rather than undergoing this ordeal however, I'd prefer to lie quietly surrounded by the odour. Because I'd got used to it, I experienced the smell as little more than a slightly heavy air. (I was helped in this by force of habit). A combination of the scent, my fatigue and an inability to move conspired to have a powerful narcotic effect on me. I dozed off again.

It must have been not long after that I was awoken again by a joyful din. This heralded the reappearance of my three beautiful girls. Accompanied by sounds of shoving and heaving, a tray of impressive proportions emerged through the hole in the floor at the top of the staircase. The tray was placed on the bed like a table and bore a number of large cups brimful with thick, wicked chocolate, a pyramid of half-cooked biscuits, pots of anchovy purée aux fines herbes, raw minced steak with spring onions and jams made from acacia flowers, nasturtiums and violets.

Justifying ourselves with the notion that we needed to restore our strength, we indulged in some serious gluttony. I remember the women nearly choked with laughter when the violet jam I was eating stained my lips and palate the same colour as that of a chow. They failed to notice the effect it had had on them of course. (I forgot to point out, by the way, that in order to stuff themselves, the three of them were totally naked, and that I too was wearing not a stitch of clothing).

The virtues of this light meal, which I'd be so bold as to describe as 'musky', soon made themselves felt. I paid my pretty little gluttons back by stuffing my cock in their mouth and then in their belly, although not very deeply. To be perfectly frank, I should point out that Viola was the only recipient of my come. I didn't want to blunt my weapon too much so early in the day.

In the wake of this storm, there was a period of repose. Then the three of us went down to the bathroom together where we found that the large bath had already been filled for us. The water probably had gas pumped through it because it fumed and fizzed like warm champagne. We managed to make our ablutions last a considerable length of time. These were made all the more delightful by the opportunity they presented for games, both innocent and perverse, for intimate exploration, amusing comparisons, disingenuousness, childlike curiosity and the satisfying of that curiosity. In short, I stepped out of the bath with my prick stiff again, my muscles taut, my head clear and my heartbeat as regular as a metronome. There's nothing like childish pursuits to restore a man's vigour. And the person I now compared myself to was not Balthazar, in whose name I had been decked out, but Solomon, the king who when he reached a venerable age was able to return to the vigour of his youth by surrendering his aged body to the lascivious revels of naked girls.

I shaved and Candida rubbed me down with a horsehair glove. Viola gave the especially sensitive parts of my body a good licking, then she powdered them with talc. The two of them helped me to dress. Just as on the day before, they threw a large cape over the brilliant clothing which I described earlier. This cape had a rather pastoral charm about it. The colour and type of material created the impression that it had been cut from a square of dead moss. After the women had clothed their nakedness in astrakhan dresses which were open at the front like Levites, and which were equal in all respects to the lustrous skin of Candida, the three of us left the room. In the courtyard, however, I took leave of my darlings. We were standing at the foot of a staircase which, they pointed out, was the one that led up to where I wanted to go.

When I reached my destination, I found nobody up there. A brisk wind was blowing. It was icy and my cape was flapping in the breeze. So I wrapped it snugly around me. Fortunately the material was thick. I walked along the watch tower and eventually reached a terrace. It was extensive although irregular in shape and situated above what I called the main living quarters, that's to say, the keep and the two small side towers.

Bordering the terrace was a parapet, quite low on the courtyard side, and it was obvious that the terrace followed the scalloped outline of the buildings which supported it, whereas on the side which overlooked the sea, it was marked out by the curve of the ramparts. Judging by my shadow on the granite flagstones, which was barely large enough to cover a rabbit, it must have been about midday. The tide had just turned. It was going out. This was evident from the direction of packets of foam, seaweed, and thin floating bodies. A buoy at the end of its chain was straining towards the open sea. But several yards of the causeway which linked the chateau to dry land were still hidden under the water. The waves gently licked around the base of the ramparts as they do against the hull of a ship in deep water. Grey birds swirled around and above, shrieking like madwomen.

'It's a little too late to see them diving,' said a voice. 'When the tide's coming in, the fish rise to the surface. Then the birds take full advantage of all the booty they can plunder from the waters.'

The man I was waiting for, no doubt forewarned by the Negroes, had come up without my hearing and stood next to me, bareheaded, his hair blowing in the wind, the rest of his body covered in a fox fur which just broke over his slippers.

Once you've had the pleasure (or misfortune) to meet Montcul, it's difficult to forget his face. I'm convinced that his victims, when they close their eyes for the last time, take the image of this man to the grave with them. His face is a little larger than expected in proportion to the rest of his body. His eyes, with straw-coloured pupils, are deep set, and overarched by thin, reddy-brown eyebrows. His nose is large, a little aquiline above the wide, twitching nostrils. His mouth is also large, with very pale lips, tightly closed yet voluptuous like the pendulous lips of the largest cats. His skin, which is almost too pale, is shaved so close and powdered so scrupulously that no hint of beard is visible. The whole is crowned by a luxuriant head of hair, mahogany and copper in colour. A parting above his left eye divides it into two waves which fall below his ears, a style popular with women and certain ridiculous pederasts (although Montcul is no pederast and he is the last person in the world one would describe as ridiculous). His neck, also feminine, is rounded at the base as in the early stages of goitre, and he's never seen wearing anything but open, or very wide silk collars. He'd have to be described as looking like a cross between a sea eagle and an Anglican vicar. And this is not the most unusual aspect of this person.

I speak of him in the present tense as if he were still alive because, in spite of what I've learnt to the contrary (and this will be recounted later) I'm not convinced he's no longer among us.

When he noticed that I was examining him from head to toe, he started to laugh.

'What do you think of our carnival then?' he asked.

I didn't know what to say in reply, so he went on:

'Please, I beg you, don't mistake me for some harmless, mad old lady who copes with the emptiness of her soul by wearing fancy-dress. On the other hand, I'd be wrong to deny that I have a rather extravagant taste for masks and all conceivable types of disguise. But that explains nothing more than the dinner you were served yesterday evening. And you may as well resign yourself to the fact that succeeding meals will be of the same order, or rather, the same *dis*order. You'll agree of course that since I've decided to retire from the world, to cut myself off from my former existence and the circles I moved in, and since in order to achieve these various ends I've become the owner of this chateau situated, as you see, on the margins of the world, a chateau which I've had rebuilt and decorated without aesthetic consideration, but with the sole aim of creating a climate of exile; you'll agree that it makes sense to do away with the sort of clothes which are worn, day in day out, in almost every corner of the globe. Besides, such clothing is rather ugly to look at, it's uncomfortable for the more delicate parts of our body and it reeks of English middle class vulgarity. The English bourgeoisie is a species whom, in the natural order of animals, I would place just above the sewer rat, or the *mus panticus* as the zoologists call it and *pantegana*, as it is known in the City of the Doges. Everybody who spends time at Gamehuche, whether of their own free will or by force, gets tricked out in this eighteenth century fantasy. Of course I don't take it seriously. And yet, to my mind, it rather suits you and it goes very nicely with my

Negroes. And the idea of these dressing gowns which the two of us are wearing under our large cloaks in the open air came to me while listening (once more) to one of the pieces of music which is most dear to me: the end of the first act of *Don Giovanni*. It's blindingly obvious that the drawings of the only Englishman who could handle a pencil or paint-brush – I'm referring to the one who's buried at Menton, in case you're racking your brains as to who it might be – it was his drawings which helped me enormously to put together my wardrobe.'

I may have made some sort of reply here, but it was without significance, and I've no particular wish to recall it. Indeed I don't wish to recall any aspect of my part in the conversation. From this point on, all I'll do is record Montcul's pronouncements (the *Montculiana*, so to speak). I make no claims as to their being set down in the exact order in which they were uttered on that particular morning. But they'll cast more than a little light on the bizarre mind of the Master of Gamehuche.

*

'I've lived in most of the great cities of Europe, above all London and Paris. I must admit that I've always been thoroughly bored by those male past-times, which from your point of view and in the sort of language you use, you'd call a 'binge', 'loose-living', 'affairs', or 'debauchery'. All too soon one comes up against the limits of such activities and I've never been able to take any real pleasure in them. Adultery under a Geraldy duvet! How sterile!

And what about those girls who when they get undressed, give off a strong scent of wildfowl? They reside in the rue Paul-Valéry, or some hospitable house in the rue du Bac, full of Siamese cats and anatomical subjects like so many ex-votos in medical plaster. What a tedious litany! There are so many men who, as a point of honour, boast of being a 'skirt chaser' or a 'lady killer'. Can't they get it into their tiny little heads that the whole point of every hunt is the *kill*? Quest, tracking, pursuit, these are the sort of words they use. But their game will never be anything more than artificial, frivolous, if it only ends up with a quick fuck after a family gathering, rather than the unleashing of the hunter on his prey.

*

Surely there's nothing more fragile than a woman's beauty. All it takes is a blade in the hand of a Negro (or in the hairy paw of an orang-utan, according to our favourite classics) and, with a few deft movements, your priceless gem, your black tulip, your goddess, your masterpiece of creation bears a close resemblance to the skinned head of a calf.

*

And what's more, how can we accept, in all honesty, that those whores who've served us can then go on and serve so many others after us? Doesn't this degree of tolerance display an unforgivable lack of spirit? Don't you think it's hopelessly at odds with the forms of pleasure we demand in other spheres? When we've enjoyed a fine fish, or a game bird, the

sense of satisfaction is heightened and we digest better if we see that the plate contains nothing but
bones picked clean. To my way of thinking, it's
exactly the same with debauchery. It simply doesn't
work unless accompanied by the physical destruction
of the creature whose only function was to provide us
with the pleasure of her body. For there's no other
way in which to truly quench the desire.

If I were capable of love, then I think I'd get mar-
ried and that my love would remain faithful in the
face of every test, even under the most painful of
torture. Mind you, love is such a disreputable word.

*

That young German woman you saw yesterday evening, I probably won't spare her. I don't really love her
and I've never thought of marrying her. However,
she and I are so alike in certain aspects that up until
now I've always spared her the worst. Besides, none
of my former whores has been able to make me come
as much as this one does. So, for her, any danger is a
long way off. But I don't think she's labouring under
the slightest misapprehension as to what awaits her
when her services are no longer required.

Later, when we're at table, remind me to tell you
the story of how she came to be at the chateau. It's
an amusing tale.'

*

During the final years I spent in the company of
men, before I donned my hermit's robes, I indulged
my fantasy by imagining and, more often than not,

carrying out a number of tasks which could be accomplished without any great difficulty. But these were ideas which unfortunately occur to no-one. Let me give you an example. Robbery is tedious, adolescent, and a bit vulgar unless it's done out of necessity, in which case there are much easier ways of earning cash legitimately. But, what about *adding* paintings to the collections at the Louvre or the National Gallery, introducing preposterous objects into the dusty and solemn order of national museums? These are innovative crimes for which, I might add, you can't be punished if the law is unaware that they're feasible, or even that they've been committed. I enjoyed inserting very expensive copies of books among the second-hand junk for sale at the booksellers on the banks of the Seine. A Sulpice Sabon edition of the *Delie* and *The Flowers of Evil* were the first. I placed fat pearls in a number of oysters and concealed the shellfish among the baskets, taking care not to be seen by the fishmonger. Most of them were very high quality. However, just for a real surprise I slipped in one or two false ones. In similar fashion, I stuffed some gold coins into the stomach of the biggest carp at the market in the quartier St Paul, which, as you know, is the Jewish quarter. Fighting broke out at the fishmonger's on the following day and two women, the mothers of several children, died in the fracas. Live eels and crayfish cropped up before high mass in the fonts of various churches, most notably Notre Dame. It was a fish soup for the verger. In contrast to these acts of generosity, an excellent outcome (as the doctors say) can often be achieved by injecting a massive dose of strychnine solution or certain prussiates into oranges or mandarins which are then tossed into the middle of a greengrocer's stall. I can also recommend the following, although this is a little joke that should not be played too often. Take a number of sharp-pointed drawing pins and after you've smeared them in curare paste, scatter them on the wooden gang-ways which lead to the bathing stations along a river.

Strengthening the hand of chance like this is a source of great joy. You'll calm the nerves, and find greater peace of mind than if you spurt a whole bucketload of spunk. And yet, I'd be prepared to wager that you won't follow my lead. The reason is, and I think again you'll be surprised by this, that I've never yet come across anybody (not even the young Princess de Warmdreck) who shares my taste and ingenuity for such undertakings.

*

I made a full list of my past and future amusements but, unfortunately for you, I haven't kept it. When I got to the very end of the list I left for Gamehuche. I'd only just finished settling in and having the cha-teau organised in accordance with my instructions, which you already know about, when the war broke out. Just in time, I must admit. It swept away the legal system and with it went most of the obstacles which would have fouled up my plans.

Of course, it was not without a certain delight that I learnt of the defeat of the English, French and Belgian armed forces and their desperate retreat to the Pyrenees. Being of sound mind, I've always enjoyed seeing soldiers of my own country fleeing for their lives. Thanks to the speed of the RAF lorries, they were easily the first to go through the check points in the region where Gamehuche stands. A few days later, the Germans arrived and they occupied the whole coast.

Because I proclaimed so loudly the hatred and disgust I felt for my country and as I'd changed my name from Mountarse to Montcul – I did this because I was outraged by the idiocy of the Battenbergs who had just changed their name to Mountbatten – the Germans, in a moment of monumental stupidity which is the very bedrock of the Germanic soul, took me for an English fascist or some such. In the end they saw me as a faithful follower of their cause and gave me their goodwill and support. At the same time I had to 'get into bed' – that's the phrase – with the head of the local resistance. The co-operation of these men – and a more imbecilic band of murderers, thieves and pimps you couldn't wish to meet – made it much easier for me to carry out my business. Now the war's over, these young bastards have torn off the mask of patriotism and it's simply as procurers that I use them. In exchange for money, or to be more precise, for a little gold coin with the effigy of a crippled Napoleon III, they provide me with whatever I need in the way of boys, girls, children or animals, and they do it with as much enthusiasm as the Neapolitans.

During the war I often received a gift-wrapped delivery of officers and soldiers whom they'd ambushed. The prisoners appeared in my shows and were the subject of my experiments. It was in the interest of the Maquis because they could get rid of them without putting themselves in jeopardy, and I also gave them a donation to their funds. I remember one big fat Colonel from Wurtemberg. We entertained ourselves by making him remove his uniform and his underwear, then, when he was stark naked, his entire body was tattooed with the same uniform. It was perfect in every detail down to his leggings, his decorations, his gold braid, his holster and every regimental button. After which, when the fellow had sucked (without biting) the Negroes' cocks and had swallowed all the come, he was dispatched by Caligula. I've always had a high regard for the Israelis who apparently, so I'm told, subjected ranking officers and Generals in the British Army to the first part of this treatment, before sending them back to their quarters thus 'decorated'. This practice should be more widespread – tattooing all professional soldiers in this manner. My only regret is that I never managed, despite the offer of a fat bounty, to procure an example of those glorious Russian generals who are loaded down with more gold and ironmongery than all the others. Just think what fun and games we'd have had, trying to engrave those huge epaulettes and a washing line of medals on their cossack hides!'

A rather lugubrious bellow from behind us put an end to M. de Montcul's semi-monologue. It was the Negro Gracchus who was bellowing and growling on a large spiralled conch shell – the signal, I was told, that lunch was served. When the trumpeter had finally run out of breath, we went down.

'I detect a slight obsession in you,' I commented to my host. 'You place such importance on the pedigree of all those whose story you tell, don't you?'

'Your observation is correct. I've never totally shrugged off that awful old English habit of talking about a "fine poodle" or a "large percheron" or a "cream Persian" rather than a dog, a horse or a cat. Everything that comes to us from our fucked-up motherlands turns us into idiots.'

And he steered me towards the dining room.

Here the decor was unchanged from the previous day, except that the candles were unlit, the hangings had been furled like sails above the large windows on the courtyard side, letting a rather gloomy light into the room. I found the company as I expected – that is to say, only Michelette was missing. She had served her purpose and the crabs had already picked her little bones clean.

We sat in the same positions as the night before, the only difference being that Montcul and Luna de Warmdreck were no longer sharing their bench with anyone. Edmonde, although she'd only just emerged from the kitchen where, according to her, she'd been working for the benefit of our bellies, was smiling and radiant. Her breasts and arse bobbed up and down under her mauve shirt. The gilded leather corset she wore, which squeezed her in severely at the waist had the effect of making both her breasts and arse larger and more beautiful.

The two blacks were coming and going with large dishes of sea urchins. At first, this filled me with delight because there's nothing I like more than the delicious orange or saffron clusters which are the eggs of this living sea food. But I was in for a disappointment because all we were given of the sea urchin was the outside shell. Each of these contained a braised lamb's testicle on a bed of pureed shallots.

While disapproving of these starters, which to my taste were detestable, I nevertheless found them witty and praised their ingenuity, for the sea urchin which is flesh coloured on the inside and covered in spiky hairs on the outside is, morphologically speaking, a cunt. This is so obvious that it might be thought of as one of Mother Nature's jokes. So there was something rather humorous about stuffing a bollock into such a place which is more usually adapted to receiving the tip of a prick.

Meanwhile, the Negroes, with pig-like expressions, were devouring the testicles and licking out the inside of the shell. Montcul, in customary fashion, was badmouthing England. He was recounting the story of one of his relatives, a Mountarse from the previous century, with whom Queen Victoria had cuckolded not only her husband, but also her principal lover – Alfred, Lord Tennyson.

'At the first broadside my uncle fired on the royal mattress,' he said, 'he sodomised her Gracious Majesty in such great style that she was overcome with delight. Especially as her Poet Laureate left a great deal to be desired in this respect. By virtue of reading the Bible and a medical dictionary, he didn't want to screw her more than once a week and nowhere other than in what he referred to as 'the vessel of highest morality' i.e. her vagina. My uncle on the other hand, who was a man proud of his prick, fucked her in every hole, and with good grace. After he'd well and truly filled her cunt, he turned his attention to her arse, her mouth, even her nostrils. Everything I'm telling you here I've read in the memoirs of my uncle, Jonathan Mountarse. These are as yet unpublished, which is a shame. But it seems that the Queen was a greedy guzzler of sperm. She used the flat of her hand to wipe anything which oozed come and collected it from all the places she'd been shafted so as to shove it afterwards down her throat, all the time braying that it tasted better than zabaglione in whisky. Also, in comparison to Mountarse spunk, Tennyson's was as thin as rice water apparently.

My uncle finished by thrashing the royal slut with his braces. In gratitude for this, she made him a knight of the Garter. I never succeeded at court to the same degree that Sir Jonathan did. I must admit – I wish to be fair in all matters – he could certainly get an erection quicker than me, and then, the arses of royalty have rarely come within range of my braces.'

He broke off to take a helping of little tongues from a dish. These tongues were so small in fact that I couldn't think they'd come from any creature other than a guinea pig. Then he continued, almost seamlessly.

'Consider, if you will, the most common object of

the British household bar none – the English teapot. You'd have to have lost all critical faculties to believe that the only use such an utensil is put to is the preparation of infusions. The shape of its spout, like a skinny prick, its round belly which our national prostitutes fill with hot water before applying it to their mound – all these point unerringly towards its ultimate purpose. The English teapot is a dildo. (I've even seen one which was sheathed with astrakhan like the loin cloth of a Zulu). And there's little doubt it will remain one till the end of time. Or until my fellow countrymen have learnt how to bring their sad womenfolk to orgasm, which is highly unlikely. Beside isn't the limbless man the ideal of every woman in the United Kingdom? He's infirm, with a big prick (a teapot again) and is available whenever they want.

Let me add, à propos this unusually suggestive shape, that the English teapot also resembles the head of a rhinoceros. I've always dreamed of possessing an animal of this species, trained to use it's horn to fuck with. I'd release the beast into the park, just when it was full of stern matrons and their little charges, and I assure you there'd be much shrieking, agitation and joy.'

He was becoming tedious with his inverted patriotism. It was like listening to the idle gossip of a frumpy old Irishwoman. So, just for a change of tune, I reminded him that he'd promised to tell me another story – about the arrival of his girlfriend, the young Princess, at Gamehuche.

'And what does the aforementioned 'young Princess' think of this?'

He fondled his neighbour's breasts without sympathy and continued:

'Are you going to answer my question, wench? It's you we're talking about.'

'The princess and the wench are at M. de Montcul's disposal, for whatever he wants to ask,' said the German woman with a sigh and a lovely movement of her neck.

'Good,' he replied. 'I'm a gallant man, and I would never have divulged the smallest piece of information without the consent of the principal character concerned. But, as you have given it, I'll begin.'

FIVE

'So, it was between the spring and summer of 1942 that I first met General Baron von Novar. He'd just been appointed commander of the air forces in lower Brittany. He heard that I, your host and servant, was a sort of English eccentric (the expression is still in use) and finding his old fatherland repugnant and at the same time being a great admirer of the new Germany, he wanted to get to know me. And very civil he was indeed (strange as that may seem, I must admit). After his aides had warned me of his impending visit, he was driven to the chateau and introduced himself to me. To the ear-splitting background noise of his motorcycle escort which was waiting on the beach until the causeway became passable for vehicles, I was given a fortunate piece of advice, namely that in order to avoid any awkward incidents I ought to use one of the towers with barred windows to conceal the two Jews who had been entrusted to my keeping by the Maquis. They'd come from a small village in the interior where they'd rather rashly taken refuge.

Because I knew what to say in order to ingratiate myself with a brute such as this, von Novar soon got to like me more than he did any of his compatriots, whom he despised as a matter of course if their rank was lower than his. This was a time when he couldn't get enough of me and he'd come to see me at

Gamehuche three or four times a week. It was customary for him to arrive in the company of his niece, the young Princess de Warmdreck, whom you see here and whom at this very moment I am fingering under her dress. The princess is pliant. The whore's laughing. He who laughs last laughs best. But I digress – to return to our bemedalled sheep.

The general conceived an almost fanatical affection for me and in a fit of trust which I'm sure I didn't merit, he let me in on the reasons as to why and how he'd brought his niece with him. The alleged pretext was that he required her services as a secretary, but the real reason for his move had been to get her out of Germany and to spare her the obligatory work and degrading conditions which were unworthy of a person of her social standing. After all, she came from a family which, before Bismarck, counted reigning princes among its ranks.

To begin with I was mildly bored by these visits which, due to the delicate balancing act I needed to perform, I obviously couldn't get out of. However, I was soon seduced by the unconscious comedy which makes preening birds of high-ranking officers and generals the world over. Von Novar's confidences no longer bored me. Besides, as I said before, he had the personality of a sheep. And also, I was beginning to look favourably on his niece. There was a third person who came with them on these visits – one whom I took little pleasure in seeing and who viewed me in a very unfriendly manner. This man was a flight lieutenant who served in the maritime squadrons of the Luftwaffe. His insignia was something like an aileron

or a fin, and he let it be known, albeit in a purely un-
official way, that he was the Princess de Luneborge's
fiancé. He was also of noble birth, top drawer in fact,
but more of a beast than a human being. He was pale
with red hair, over six foot tall and there was a strong
odour of the kennel about him. Perhaps he used too
much pyrethra shampoo. Whenever he got an erection it was displayed ostentatiously. (Military trousers and those short flying jackets are cut delib-
erately to show this off). And you didn't need to be a
clairvoyant, or a chaplain, to see that the whore of a
niece was creaming herself for him. It was clear that
his fat cock had intimate knowledge of her best
places. Moreover, at the risk of repeating myself, I
had an image of those places in my own head (and
groin) rather as one has an intensely sharp image of
St Peter's in Rome, or the Invalides or an as yet
unknown brothel.

The weather got hotter and hotter as the summer
wore on. The general sometimes sent a staff car to
take me from Gamehuche to a deserted beach near
Saint-Quoi-de-Vit. The three of them often went
swimming there, guarded by the motorcycle escort
who were posted stiffly at the foot of a dune. Von
Novar sheltered under a parasol and chattered on
with such innocence that you didn't need to listen
to him with any greater attention than you pay to
the sound of soughing shingle. Luneborge lay
bronzing in the sun. Then, quite peony-red and
silent, she'd plunge into the water and swim with a
powerful, relaxed stroke out to sea. She was followed a little way behind by that bastard whom I

hated: flight-lieutenant Conradin. I was sure the fiancés were fucking each other in the water – this is a delightful exercise, actually. Let me give you the approved method: the woman lies out flat and the man positions himself underneath. Then guiding his stiff prick into the hole of his choice, he can fuck or bugger the woman with powerful thrusts of his hips. This has to be done brutally if the salt water fails to provide good lubrication. All that then remains is to surrender oneself to the movement of the waves, which support your back like cradling hands under a hammock. But a word of warning! Don't forget that any clothing you remove at the beginning of this operation, swimsuit or trunks, should be put round your neck if you don't want to risk losing them.

When they returned, after an hour or more, breathing heavily, their faces strained with fatigue, I felt envious of that man. The whore slumped onto the sand, worn out, as if she had serviced an entire squad of infantry men. Immediately her eyelids lowered to cover those placid aquamarine eyes which you see before you. I know of nothing designed to provoke one to great excess than the emptiness of such deep-set pale blue eyes in a well-tanned face. She dried her beautiful hair in the sun, including the wonderful hazel hair of her armpits which she displayed without shame. He, I noticed, slid his hand underneath her and was gently fondling her buttocks. The bastard was getting horny again doing this and she, with a light swelling of her neck and belly, showed that she was not insensitive to it. Fucking hell! I swore that before long I'd use the slut as a container for my shaft.

The boys in the Resistance were informed of my wishes and it was pointed out what enormous benefit would accrue to them the day they brought my three victims to me in good shape. They devised a plan of attack, and it was carried out on the day after Midsummer's day.

The heat that morning was intense and inevitably it drove my quarry to the beach. Meanwhile I gave fire-jumping, round dances and other exhausting activities from the day before as an excuse for not leaving the chateau.

The sun was hot enough to crack the pebbles along the shoreline and it beat down ferociously on close-cropped Germanic heads. Consequently the escort, who like good soldiers slept standing up at their post, were stretched out on the sand before they even knew what had hit them. They weren't so much grievously wounded as stunned, by pellets fired silently from air rifles which were supplied from my own private arsenal. The three principal figures had just got dressed as the weather that morning was too hot even for them. If my henchmen had arrived half an hour later, they'd have found the beach empty.

As any resistance was futile, they were captured, tied up gagged and hooded, and thrown into the back of a cart between two beds of seaweed where they lay like fresh lobsters. The Maquisards then returned to the (none too seriously) wounded. Since the tide was coming in, they were stripped naked and simply buried up to their necks in the damp sand with their arms strapped to their sides. This was done about fifty yards from the nearest wave, thereby allowing them plenty of time to contemplate the rising tide before being overwhelmed by its eddies. I'm of the opinion that death by drowning in this way, with the lapping waves, the foam and the ebb and flow, must cause a man's nervous system to go haywire. His rational faculties must fall apart, like one who dies under the lash. On the other hand, perhaps it was over-indulgent to deal in this way with such pitiful creatures as ordinary Luftwaffe rank and file.

As for the prisoners, when their 'chaperons' were removed – do allow me this falconry term – they found themselves in this very room and it was late afternoon. The curtains were drawn, all the candles were ablaze, although outside it was still broad daylight and the heat was overwhelming. The Maquisards had slipped away, back to their heathland and their little meadows, as soon as they had pocketed their gold coins.

Look around you and you'll see the theatre in which the drama unfolded – the only difference being that it's now lit by daylight. So, let's give a brief résumé of the actors, victims and walk-on parts, the characters who were to perform.

On one side we had the foreigners, General von Novar, flight lieutenant Conradin and the Princess de Warmdreck. The two men were in army uniform, but wearing espadrilles which were not regulation issue. Luneborg, barefooted, was dressed in a short orange beach dress which showed off to perfection her

102

brown shoulders, her armpits, her legs and provided an interesting glimpse of her breasts.

On the other side we had the inmates of the chateau. Firstly the master of the household, your humble servant. On this particular occasion, he was wearing a black Cashmere dressing robe with a violet sash around his waist. This made him look rather like 'His Grace, Monseigneur de Gamehuche'. Stark naked under this robe, he wore black suede slippers with violet heels. On his right and on his left were two daughters of the black race, our young friends Viola and Candida. They were also stark naked beneath long dresses, one mauve, the other vivid pink. Slashed down the front and unhooked, these were made from the skins of Tibetan goats which have hair as soft as a woman's. The high-heeled red court shoes these two tarts were wearing accentuated the length of their legs. The two Negroes, Gracchus and Publicola, were bare-chested and bare-footed. They were dressed in nothing but clinging shorts – one white satin, the other crimson – which came below their knees in the style of Neapolitan fishermen. To complete their costume, or to give them something to do with their hands, each one bore a large bunch of asparagus on a silver dish. Monseigneur de Gamehuche would be absent-mindedly sucking on a tip from time to time.

The company was completed by the only two characters whom you won't know (with good reason) – namely two Jews, John-Henry Rotschiss, formerly a metal dealer, and Simon Vert, a dentist. These two were wearing Capuchin habits, in that well-known shit colour. (The reason I gave for forcing them into such a disguise was for their own protection). Their livid complexion, the sheen of their greasy, sweaty skin, went with the habit as perfectly as leaves of sorrel under the belly of a shad.

And, now, without further ado, let the play begin.

The prisoners looked at each other and around the room. They looked at me, blinking and in some astonishment. They reminded me of nocturnal creatures caught in the beam of a torch. Then, one assumed, the men remembered they were at war, they were officers, aristocrats and Prussians, because they stiffened in that well-known manner which is a sort of morose erection. The girl on the other hand, languid, squirmed like a frightened little otter.

The general was the first to speak. It was the privilege of his rank. He told me I'd be shot, and that he'd show me how heroes in his country die.

'Wrong on two counts, my dear general. I will not be shot, because none of your men will know that it was here, in this crab hole, that your career was brought to a long overdue end. And moreover, this has nothing to do with you dying a hero's death as it's done in your country, or in any other for that matter. This is all about me enjoying the spectacle of your degradation and dishonour, and the torture that will be visited upon you. Come, my Hebrew brothers, I deliver the general into your hands. Deal with him as you will.'

I gave him a double twist of the nose, kicked him in the balls and pushed him towards the Jews. As soon as these two had first caught a glimpse of the uniforms worn by the men who were invariably their executioners, they'd run away and hidden behind the colonnade. Now they emerged, at a trot, and began to grin so ferociously and so horribly that if it hadn't been for their usefulness as instruments of torture, I'd have had them sent away before attacking the Germans myself.

They took hold of the general and struck him, slapped him on the back, pawed his body with their damp hands, groped his fat and his lean parts, but without undressing him.

Now it was the flight lieutenant's turn. I called his fiancée over to me and held her underneath the arms. She lifted her elbow obligingly to reveal her bosom which was naked and unconstrained beneath her dress.

'Undress this pig,' I told the Negroes.

He had a fine, athletic, brutal body, almost hairless, as is often the case with this type of tanned Northern male. I scrutinised it with a mixture of hate and pleasure casting a critical eye over his tool which hung between his thick-skinned balls.

'He's limp,' I said to Luna. 'Make him hard.'

The pretty little slut smiled, at the same time pretending to be confused. She went and caressed the lieutenant's undercarriage. He looked at her with repressed fury. She managed to get his organ half-erect then finished off her task by licking him expertly. I took advantage of her position to pull down her shorts and triumphantly fondle the beautiful twin globes of her arse right in front of her fiancé's eyes all the while fingering her crack. I then shoved my cock deep inside her.

'Good,' I said, a little slyly, as she turned coaxingly to offer me her face, her eyes closed, her half-open mouth, her whore's tongue. 'But to my mind there's something insubordinate about this thick foreskin. I wish to punish it. My Hebrew friends, leave the general alone and fetch the scissors. You're going to circumcise the airman.'

The victim's wrists were bound by the simple expedient of a cord which was attached to a ring above his head and pulled tight to make the operation easier. The circumcision took place and this produced a length of skin like a cannelloni, a little blood, and a certain amount of whimpering and trembling from the subject. My curiosity was well and truly aroused because I'd never seen a circumcision before. And I was pleased to record a similar curiosity not only in Viola and Candida, but also in the victim's fiancée. From that moment on I knew I wouldn't be as severe on her as on the other two. As for the circumcision, I must admit I found it disappointing. It was a show for the girls.

Laughing fit to burst, Simon Vert showed the victim the foreskin he'd just removed. He raised it to his mouth and pretended to find it tasty.

'Let's finish with the pilot,' I said. 'Little Rotschiss is going to bugger him, after which the dentist will eat his balls. And if he doesn't swallow every bit, he's a dead man.'

A length of rope was used to bring the fighter pilot's back passage within reach of the Jew. It avoided the necessity of the latter standing on cushions because he was a bit of a short arse in comparison to the German. Gracchus, on my orders and despite some whining, removed the monk's habit from the Jew. There was no mistaking the fact that the bum of my big Aryan bastard held no attraction for him, judging by the way his stubby dick flopped down like the tongue of a panting dog. I tried frightening him into an erection and Viola and Candida manhandled him, but without success. As a last resort we decided to call upon a splendid recipe of Gracchus's. After he had slapped mustard on the glans and inserted a strong red pepper into his arsehole, he flagellated him for five minutes with birch rods soaked in vinegar.

His prick stiffened (as slender as a cheap fountain pen) and although, according to Gracchus, the effect of the pepper doesn't wear off quickly, the Jew was doubtless terrified that his cock would wilt. So he slipped it into the hole without delay or the slightest difficulty, which just goes to show how well an airman's arsehole is adapted to penile entry. We laughed at the sight of the arrogant pilot being ridden by Rotschiss, while, in front of his nose, his fiancee was flicking her tongue in and out of my ear and I was openly frigging her. The Jew had climbed onto the German like a little spider on a long water fly, and was swaying back and forth. After a brief period on his swing, he ejaculated. He was lowered in order to let his prick slide out and so that Simon Vert could show just how good his teeth were.

My death threat had so terrified the dentist that it

would have required much more than mustard and a pepper to give him a hard-on. But the role I'd assigned him was not beyond his capacity as he could play it successfully with a limp dick. He swooped down on Conradin's nether regions and this time the German shrieked like a cageful of parrots. The Jew bit furiously at the scrotum bracing himself with his hands on the German's thighs. By dint of twisting and ripping, he tore out first one bollock, then the other. Eating them was more difficult. The raw balls of an adult male are tough meat, you know. And yet he managed it very quickly, almost without chewing, by pushing them down his throat with a finger. When he'd finished, his face had turned blue, like that of a hanged man. Bravo, Mr Dentist!

The victim was bleeding like a stuck pig. The boring thing about these pastimes is that they finish up making a mess all over the place. I gave the Negroes a signal and they finished him off by strangulation, then carted him out for us.

'Oh fuck it!' his fiancée said nicely. 'I should have tried a bit of testicle. But let's see what you have in store for my uncle.'

General von Novar had been stiffly contemplating our pleasures. He managed to maintain till the bitter end the bearing of a soldier, and he gave a Nazi salute to the remains of his brother-in-arms. When I called him forward, he presented himself and clicked his heels, although the rope soles produced a rather muffled sound.

I gave the order that his shoes and socks be removed. This was carried out by the Negresses who simpered and ruffled his grey hair. As the General's jacket came no lower than the hollow of his thighs, it presented no more of an obstacle to our endeavours than those short jackets worn by whores in high-class brothels, which it resembled. So it was left on. But the Negresses undid all the buttons on it and tore the shirt off in strips.

'You won't be needing it again,' I said, as his gaze lingered sadly on these rags. 'Down on all-fours.'

He obeyed. I stamped on his fingers with the heel of my shoe. I gave him a blow to the back of his neck and a couple of stinging slaps. His niece, sticking close to me, hit him twice mockingly on the nose then she pulled up her shirt so that I could finger her and lick her in front of him. While all that was going on, the Jews had set upon the corpse of the flight lieutenant which they had dragged to the back of the room as if to bring us – i.e. the general, his niece, the Negroes and I – closer together as a family. The whore moved away and went to fondle the testicles under the belly of the gold braided creature.

'The blows are getting him excited,' she said, spitting on his forehead. 'He's starting to get a little stiffy.'

She was so delightfully wanton that I was struck by an almost brotherly affection for her. She lifted her arms, in compliance with Viola's wishes who'd come up behind her to remove her dress and lick the crack between her buttocks. She was naked now and I took hold of her again. With one hand I pushed my fingers into her sopping vagina. With the other, I gently sodomised her. She sighed. It was then that my prick began to stir.

'I want you naked,' I ordered the Negroes. 'Publicola is going to fuck the general up the arse.'

I didn't have to issue such an order twice. The erectile power of those two buggers had to be seen to be believed. At the first word, at the slightest provocation, their large pricks were up, jutting out like curtain rods in black armoured steel or like the cannons of a privateer. Publicola's member, powered mercilessly by his thighs, was sunk up to his hairy balls into the eye of the Cyclops, while the Negro bent forward like a scythe blade over the German general to bite the nape of his neck. During the course of this operation, I continued my finger exercises on the interesting regions of the young princess. My reward for this was twofold – I could feel the various juices she was secreting, and on my part, I developed a powerfully erect tool.

'At last,' I said. 'We'll have some fucking.'

I threw off my Bishop's robe, which fell to the floor in front of the general. My fist thudded into the Prussian's nose – the purpose being to ensure the maintenance of my erection – and I pushed my new lover down onto the robe. She submitted to this willingly, without even feigning the slightest unease, so fascinated was she by the proportions of my prick and in particular its great battle banner – the orange and purple crest which, as you know, is my pride and joy.

With one stroke I penetrated the princess so deep that the tip of my prick touched the point which is

known in Italian as 'the fish's head'. The cunt of a
virgin this was not. But my ramrod was too engorged
not to feel constricted in there and the tart, who has
very well-developed muscles you know, squeezed me
in a most gracious manner by contracting and releas-
ing her 'nutcracker' in time to the rhythm I set up. In
short, I fucked her twat for several minutes without
coming before I withdrew, turned her over and
fucked her in the arse for about the same length of
time. Again I withdrew without coming at the very
moment Publicola, whose spunk is much more
stringy than mine, spurted his load into Novar's
guts.

After another punch to the face, and a couple of
slaps from Luna, the general obliged me by sucking
my prick which was still smeared with his niece's
shit. He performed this act assiduously and submis-
sively, in a measured way. The thought of biting did
not, I think, enter his head. Just as well. In my turn,
I buggered the general. I fucked his insides rather
roughly for nearly ten minutes without ejaculating.
Simultaneously, just to occupy my hands, I masturbated Viola and Candida, while Luna, behind me,
was rubbing her cunt up against my anus in
simulated sodomy. She also had her arms on my
shoulders and was viciously twisting her uncle's ears.
Withdrawing again, with my weapon still loaded, I
presented my besmirched dick to the general (this
time it was his own shit) with the intention of clean-
ing it in his mouth. While he was performing this act
of fellatio, which I found as sweet as a course of
game between the fish and the roast, I had him

buggered by Gracchus. The latter was not slow in filling the former's gut with the produce of his balls. But his cock remained hard and he carried on fucking.

Luna was so pale, with dark rings around her eyes in her bloodless face, that I feared the worst, or hoped for the best. She was rubbing herself against me in hysterical fashion, her legs spread in an undignified posture, the lips of her sex wide open, giving off wafts of saffron and mushroom vinegar. Her engorged clitoris was so hard that I could feel it against the small of my back like a child's finger. Looking to put her uncle's eyes out, she had latched brutally onto his forehead and eyelids. As for me I was getting more and more excited. With the general bent over sucking my penis, as if he were at prayer, the insignia and medals on his jacket were tickling the inside of my thighs and it seemed as if a thick red cloud was rising from the floor to surround myself, the princess, the Negro and the German with the effect of obscuring the four of us from the gaze of ordinary mortals and providing a setting fit for an orgy or a clash of gods or demons. For the last time, the Negro discharged a load into von Novar's arse. He grabbed him by the neck with his strangler's hands and let out a laugh which echoed round about like the thunderous outbursts of an Olympian climax. Then I pulled my cock from the victim's mouth and took hold of a cognac bottle by the neck. After slugging back a good glassful, I hit the general so hard in his gob that he lost three teeth. Luna, the ravishing shrew, tore the bottle out of my grasp, drank half the contents at one go, broke a fragment against the ring and disfigured her uncle by thrusting the jagged edge twice into his face. Then she fell on me and sucked greedily on my prick, dribbling cognac from her mouth. I grabbed hold of her at the same time and we rolled on the floor in a frenzy of sucking and licking. I bit her pubes which were smeared with female fuck juice and alcohol. I buried my mouth and nose into her vagina while her head bobbed up and down on my cock with a motion which could only be described as a furious paroxysm. Finally I came. I released floods of semen into the throat of my divine whore, who swallowed it all, like an angel. I began to go weak. My head started spinning. Just before I passed out I managed to issue a final order to the Negroes.

'Finish off the general.'

When I came round I saw that my orders had been faithfully carried out. The corpses of the two Germans were lying under the colonnade and the slut, the object of my desire, was still naked, curled up in my arms and gazing at me in tender admiration, as if she were truly in love with me.

SIX

A long silver dish was borne around the room on a small carriage pulled by Edmonde. The dish must have cost a small fortune as M. de Montcul had had it moulded specially using the body of a beautiful young girl, one whose memory he wished to honour in this concrete way. In the dish was a motley selection of desserts – little ginger tarts, rolls stuffed with garlic, onion, honey and poppy seeds, choux en pâte, lightly cooked, walnuts coated in pistachio sugar, mushroom confits, bittersweet melons and red roses fried in lambs' fat. We helped ourselves and we ate in silence. It was a weighty dessert after the story we'd just heard. However, our host, who had drunk an immoderate amount while he was recounting the events described above, was perhaps stung by our silence. All of a sudden a rush of blood coloured his face (very pale skin is susceptible to such visible changes) and he informed us that we should be wary of his anger, as we probably had little idea of exactly what sort of place we were eating in.

'The chateau de Gamehuche,' he bawled, 'is an enormous stunted prick, which is always erect and could ejaculate at any moment. Its balls are the vast cellars hollowed out of the rock on which it stands, and they're stuffed with explosives stolen first from the Germans and later from the English and

Americans. Whole truckloads went down there and the carcasses are rusting in the sea. Under our feet there's more detonating matter than in the combined magazines of three battleships. There are tons of high-explosive, the most destructive, inflammable and volatile material invented by man, whose sinister genius has always performed marvels in this arena. Do you know that all I have to do is light the wick of a particular candle, to pull on a particular rope, to press a particular button and the whole fucking lot would go up in one glorious ejaculation which would starch the sky like a convict's shirt? And I will do it. I swear I'll do it — the first time I get a hard-on but find myself incapable of shooting sperm. The detonation of Gamehuche will be an act of revenge for my own personal failure.'

The blacks, both men and women, had fled at the beginning of this rant. They were more terrified by the tone of their master's voice and his brutal gestures than by the meaning of his speech, which probably eluded them. Luna, bent over him, was trying to calm him down, speaking softly (or blowing hotly) in his ear. Edmonde took my hand saying that it would be best to leave them alone. However, before we'd left the room Montcul called after me again:

'This evening, at eight thirty. Be on the ramparts. Don't forget. You'll witness an interesting experiment.'

SEVEN

I had no trouble persuading Edmonde to take refuge in my room, but the two of us were so stuffed after the heavy meal (the other dishes included suckling pig roasted live, using the famous recipe of the Neapolitan, Della Porta, who cooked goslings live) that we fell sleep like little children. The first thing I was fortunate enough to see on waking, an hour or two later, was this woman's large and beautiful arse. She had done me the honour of placing it less than a centimetre away from my nose.

She choose a certain elixir from the chest, informing me it was quintessence of celery. After two glasses of this I was unremittingly stiff, like a ramrod. Until evening I had my partner adopt every position I could think of. I took advantage of her in every way. I fucked her in every place and in all the orifices that her body offered with inexhaustible generosity. She pandered to all my whims, harmful or benign, like a well-trained bitch. But when it came to discussing Montcul, she showed the greatest timidity. Despite running the gamut from entreaties to threats, I failed to get her to divulge the smallest detail about her master or to tell me anything about how she'd come to the chateau. Her obstinate silence on this matter confirmed my belief that she must have been kidnapped and brought here against her will.

Round about eight o'clock, we washed each other down following the delightful practice customary at Gamehuche. The very cold water we used restored my head and nerves, which to me it seemed were feeling a little out of sorts. However, the cold water had no effect on my priapic state which remained solid. My hard-on was continuing unabated despite the excesses I had visited upon the body of Edmonde. And she, admitting that perhaps I'd drunk too much 'quintessence', advised me that when I got dressed I strap my prick in a vertical position using my belt, since that was no other way of bending it. I took her advice. She brought me some tight-fitting, black silk knee-breeches. These clearly emphasised the vertical arrow which reached up as far as my navel, although a long jacket or short cape in velvet of the same colour with pale embroidery was long enough to maintain some standard of decency – if such a virtue could be said to inhabit any nook or cranny of this singular chateau. When she'd finished adjusting my dress, Edmonde kissed me and told me that I was to go up to the ramparts without her as, fortunately, she hadn't been invited to witness the experiment which was to take place that day. I wouldn't find the Negresses up there either.

In the event, the only member of the tribal family present was Gracchus, who was walking back and forth from one side of the terrace to the other, wearing that bad-tempered expression which he took on whenever I was present without the master of the house. With him was a woman whom I hadn't seen before. She was sitting on the slightly raised balustrade and had her back to the sea. Despite the melancholic aspect of her features, I reckoned she hadn't yet turned twenty. She shot a fearful glance in my direction then looked down towards a child of seven or eight months which she was holding tightly. Where had they come from, these two? I thought it could only have been from one of the towers with the barred windows, near the carriage entrance.

The first time I saw the terrace it had been empty. Now it was littered with objects like an illusionist's theatre. The objects had no perceptible shadow because of the lateness of the hour. But the smallest detail of objects and people stood out in tremendously sharp relief. This was due to the extraordinarily diffuse light which bathes the coast at the end of fine sunny days, when the light lingers so long it seems to be struggling to fade. And I could distinguish tiny subtleties and differences in each colour. Montcul couldn't have chosen a better time and place for his experiment.

A piece of apparatus which stood at the centre of the paved area (indicated by a lozenge of darker flagstones) resembled a cross of St Andrew in a vertical frame. It aroused my curiosity because of the bizarre array of belts, pulleys and levers which adorned it. But I failed to come up with any rational explanation as to its function or use. A smaller frame, furnished with more delicate belts, and standing opposite the first, resembled a salon trapeze. There were also two large ebony and black leather armchairs, rather bat-like at that crepuscular hour, and then, on an astrakhan cushion dyed strawberry pink, lay an ancient cut-throat razor. It must have been valuable because it comprised a damascened blade attached to an ornately wrought gold handle. The gold, lying against the pink fur, brought to mind perhaps the contrast between a row of teeth and inflamed gums and left a markedly unpleasant impression on me.

I was still under the effects of this impression, when I saw Montcul arrive with Publicola who was wearing nothing but breeches in coarse red cloth. One leg of the breeches was cut off at the knee, the other half-way down his thigh. My host was wrapped in a large capuchin cloak. The grey-mauve colour of the material together with his pale eyes gave him the appearance less of a fantastic monk than of an enormous and deeply unsettling moth.

'Ah,' he said in his bombastic tone, 'Let me introduce the subjects of this experiment. This is Mme Auguste Valentin. As she's among family, we'll call her by her Christian name: Berenice. She's the young wife of a Bordeaux lawyer who had to defend my interests and who acquitted himself most successfully. And this is their only son, Cesarion, in whom so many noble hopes have been invested that I really do feel sorry when I think that soon they're all to be cruelly dashed and that he will come to nothing. But, what's to be done? Sacrifices have to be made in the pursuit of knowledge. I noticed them while taking a walk on the Quinconces in Bordeaux. I informed my band of good-for-nothings, who promptly abducted them. (Ever since the end of the war they've been left with an unbearable nostalgia for this sort of undertaking). Mother and child were delivered to me a few days before your arrival. I've taken care to keep them fresh, so they might provide you with a show.'

The woman he was referring to was listening with fervent attention. She stared at us fixedly, but did not utter a sound, and in fact I was never to hear the sound of her voice. Simply, the more Moncul held forth, the greater the tenderness and fear with which she embraced her child.

Berenice Valentin was a very attractive young woman, French-looking, but more Touraine than Gasconne. She had regular features and her face was framed by chestnut hair which fell almost to her shoulders. Her eyes were the colour of cornflowers. Her little white dress gave a glimpse of a slender figure, which would undoubtedly have touched the heart of one who was sensitive to such things. Her legs were bare and tanned. She was wearing tennis shoes.

'Unfortunately, such beautiful subjects are rare,' the master of the chateau continued. 'My research is restricted to very young wives, who must not only be chaste beyond doubt but also the mother of an only child less than ten months old. It's not easy to come across a sufficient number of specimens which satisfy all these conditions. An occasion like today, which will be a feast for the eyes, is rare. Now you'll see what this experiment consists in.'

Once again he issued an order. The two Negroes took hold of the young woman and tore the child from her grasp. This was achieved without a cry, but not without resistance. After they'd thrown the brat into a corner, they led their subject to the cross of St Andrew and placed her with her back to the wood. She was bound very tightly by the wrists and ankles to the four corners of the cross and her head was placed against a board with a collar at the centre of the apparatus. When they had finished, and she could obviously move no part of her body except the middle, they picked up the child and they stripped him of all the clothing he was wrapped in. Then they suspended him by the hands from the sort of trapeze I mentioned before, opposite the cross. The mother's face and the child's were at exactly the same height and looking directly at each other.

'Good,' said the master. 'Now, bring the trapeze a little closer.'

It was brought closer, thereby giving the mother a perfectly clear sight of her unfortunate son. And when all was ready, Gracchus had the insolence to put his hand up her skirt and stroke her.

'As per normal,' Montcul said to him. 'You'll stand behind this woman and force her to keep her eyes open. She may take it into her head to close them, and then all our work will have been in vain.'

Montcul and I sat down in the armchairs less than a metre away from the scene.

'Off you go, Caligula. You know what you have to do.'

The big Negro bent down and pick up the razor. Then, almost dancing, he approached the two victims who had obviously been prepared for some sort of operation. I didn't yet know what it would be, but I guessed it would be cruel.

126

First he pawed the body of Berenice Valentin, brutally groping her breasts and thighs. Then he fixed her with his gaze and let out an evil laugh. His prick was as stiff as a crowbar inside his wide breeches. I expected to see him fall on the trembling woman, who, given the way she was tied up, was defenceless in the face of any assault. But it was towards the child that he turned. Having traced a line with his finger down the middle of the little face, he placed the edge of his weapon at the top of this line and with a precision and lightness of movement, holding his victim in a solid grip, quickly split the skin of the forehead, the nose (with its cartilage) the lips, the gums, and the chin down to the base of the neck. He continued down through the chest, the belly and finally the tiny penis which was carefully divided into two strictly equal parts. Blood was spurting from everywhere, horribly. Then the Negro, with his long nails, took hold of the two sides of the wound at the point where the nose had been and pulled the skin violently to the left and right. In a matter of seconds he had flayed the child in front of the mother's eyes. The operation was repeated lower down, with the effect of skinning the whole of the little body inside out as far as the thighs. The mother, whose eyes had been held forcibly open by the other Negro, had taken in every detail of the terrible operation. The noise of her breathing rose and fell like the heaving sea. Instead of the deathly pallor which might have been expected, her cheeks had taken on a tinge of purple, which curiously echoed the hideous appearance of the little flayed body.

'At this moment in a woman's life,' said Montcul. 'When she's still tied to her offspring by a sort of phantom umbilical cord, think of the shock (hardly an adequate description) that's caused by seeing the face of her only child destroyed instantly in front of her, this face which is the object of all her love, which is the site of every reason she has for living, the only object or image for which she feels any real emotion, to see it as if erased in a moment before her eyes, transformed into an anatomical drawing. Just think of it! You must admire me for having invented such an instrument of shock. If the nervous system behaved like molecules in a chemical reaction, what sort of response would we expect? But human nature is absurd, and the most common reaction almost defies belief. Generally, as you'll see, this gets them hot.'

Caligula had plunged the blade into the little boy's chest who was still breathing, I think. Then after he had released him, without even moving away from us, with an energetic gesture, hurled him over the balustrade.

'Bye bye, crab meat,' he said.

The razor blade was scrupulously cleaned on a fold in his shorts and returned to its furry bed. After this the executioner set about his work once more. He grabbed hold of the mother's dress, tore all her underwear into strips, without undoing the cords which bound her. Her beautiful body was completely exposed. It was a little fuller than I'd imagined, and it was burning, crimson and blotchy like a measles rash. Gracchus was manipulating the levers and tipped the cross so that it assumed a horizontal position at the base of the frame – a fold-away bed where our victim lay available to all and sundry. Caligula, who had removed his breeches with one swift movement was sporting a magnificent hard-on. He leant over the beautiful woman bound by her hands and legs and with one finger opened up her cunt which was mossy with tawny hair and bathed in bodily fluids. He placed the tip of his prick at the opening. Then with one thrust of his hips, he buried his tool up to the balls in the soft flesh. It was as enormous as I remembered it from the day before when he brandished it like a club over the back of Michelette's neck.

'Now, watch this closely,' Montcul said.

Leaning towards the face of Berenice, he also took her pulse. Her features were completely wayward, her eyes wide open, and she opened her frothing mouth which she tendered with a sort of despair towards the lips of the man who was fucking her with arched back as if he wanted to avoid contact with every part of her body except the inside of her vagina. Her nipples were growing into points as hard as armour, her stomach rose and fell, a shiver, which ended in a convulsion, ran over her skin. There was no doubt that she was in the grip of a blind and violent orgasm.

'At the first onslaught,' continued my host, 'without any need for foreplay, the whore has an orgasm. And this was a frigid woman, you know. Even in the arms of her beloved husband, I don't think she ever got wet. But they're all the same. Treat them in the way I have and they come like bitches. Look at those contortions, her eyes rolled back in her head, that ecstatic expression . . . fuck me! I'm certain you have a hard-on, especially you, who's so proud of his prick, apparently.'

He touched me, then fell silent for about a minute, deep in thought. Then, with sudden hostility:

'Go down, now. You've seen enough. Go and sate your vulgar desire on that large arse which I know you're so fond of, or on the mounds of my Negresses. We'll finish without you.'

I obeyed his order without hesitation and made myself scarce. Not that I had any intention of rejoining the girls, who were hiding somewhere or other. After what I'd witnessed, I'd have been incapable of any courtesy towards them. No, I departed because, quite apart from any judgement I might make on what my redoubtable friend called his 'experiments', I was terrified by his capriciousness, his abrupt changes of mood, to such an extent that were I to stay any longer at the chateau I feared the worst.

I went up to my room and changed out of my Gamehuche costume into one which was generally more acceptable in European countries. Without delay, and without worrying about a suitcase I couldn't find, I made a dash for my car. The engine started up at the first time of asking. Gracchus, who had immediately appeared in the courtyard, was watching me and this time there was something about his expression which made me think he envied me. I was worried that he might not open the gates for me, but no sooner had I asked him to do so than he complied.

Unfortunately, I saw that as the tide had been rising for the last two hours, the sea had completely covered the causeway. But such was my desire to get out of the oppressive enclosure, to break the circle, that I had no hesitation in driving my car out of the chateau onto the platform outside. The gates were closed behind me. That was the last I saw of any of them.

I spent all night hunched over the steering wheel, watching and waiting for the waters to reach their highest point, then recede again. Dawn came and by about six o'clock the waves were no longer breaking over the road. The wind was so strong when I crossed the causeway that I had difficulty steering straight. For some time I drove round aimlessly on the poor roads of the hinterland, and when I found a sheltered spot with a copse, I stopped the car, wound up all the windows and slept the sleep of the dead.

EIGHT

I can't say I was wholly surprised, three weeks after I'd got home, to read the following paragraph which appeared in the miscellaneous section of *Le Phare de Vit*. (This was the newspaper I'd subscribed to a little before I left in order to find out the times of the tide).

"Yesterday towards nightfall, an explosion of extraordinary violence caused consternation in our region. A terrifying vertical flash seemed to light up the sky to the south of Saint-Quoi. At the same time, houses shook and an unprecedented boom spread panic among the populace and their cattle. A number of theories have been put forward to explain the origin of this phenomenon – An atomic test? An accident caused by smugglers? – which seems to have occurred in the most deserted region of the Côte de Vit."

A few days later, a longer article confirmed what I'd already guessed, namely that the source of the mysterious explosion was Gamehuche. Not the slightest trace of the chateau or its inhabitants had been found. Neither high tide nor low tide had thrown anything up. The place which I had known as luxurious and fortified was now nothing more than a vast jumble of stones, soon to be a home to seaweed and shellfish. The journalist wrote in glowing terms of the owner of the chateau who had vanished, whom he described in turn as M. de Mountarse, *Montcul* as he was known in the Resistance, a wealthy Englishman, a philanthropist, a democrat, an exemplary patriot, and a loyal friend of France. His article ended with a fervent appeal to readers to subscribe towards the cost of a bust of the hero which would be erected in front of the town hall at Saint-Quoi.

There seems little doubt, (and it was probably during the course of a new experiment, given the time of the explosion) that Montcul had got an erection but failed to find anything capable of making him come. And so, faithful to his promise, I think he pushed the button and blew the whole fucking lot sky high. I sent a small donation to the subscription fund as one last salute to this man of intolerable grandeur. It was done in a spirit of humour which I'm sure he'd have liked.

In order that my terrible narrative might at least end on a note of tenderness, I should state that, often when I close my eyes, at the same time I conjure up an image of Edmonde's arse. Very quickly it appears in the dark sky behind my eyelids, floating like a pink and white hot air balloon. When I see that it's aiming friendly little farts at me from between its quivering roundness, I smile and think of that dear sweet woman whose greatest ornament it was.

However, neither the pink nor the white will ever erase from my mind those words of Montcul's:

'Eros is a dark god.'